D1384446

THE MCCAFFERTYS: RANDI

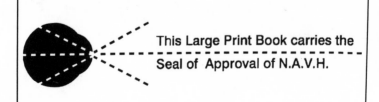

This Large Print Book carries the
Seal of Approval of N.A.V.H.

THE MCCAFFERTYS: RANDI

LISA JACKSON

WHEELER PUBLISHING

An imprint of Thomson Gale, a part of The Thomson Corporation

THOMSON

✦

™

GALE

Detroit • New York • San Francisco • New Haven, Conn. • Waterville, Maine • London

THOMSON
GALE

LIBRARY OF CONGRESS CATALOGING-IN-PUBLICATION DATA

Jackson, Lisa.
   The McCaffertys — Randi / by Lisa Jackson.
      p. cm. — (The McCaffertys series ; #4) (Wheeler Publishing large print romance)
   First published as: Best-kept lies. Harlequin, c2004.
   ISBN-13: 978-1-59722-569-4 (lg. print : alk. paper)
   ISBN-10: 1-59722-569-X (lg. print : alk. paper)
   1. Large type books. I. Title. II. Title: Randi.
PS3560.A223M364 2007
813'.54—dc22   2007015818

Published in 2007 by arrangement with Harlequin Books S.A.

Printed in the United States of America on permanent paper
10 9 8 7 6 5 4 3 2 1

Dear Reader,

I think this is a fabulous idea! One of my most popular series, THE McCAFFERTYS, is being republished.

When the first book of the miniseries, *The McCaffertys: Thorne,* came out, I received a lot of letters and tons of e-mail asking questions about *The McCafferty* brothers and their wayward younger sister. With each new book in the series, I received more and more mail. The sexy, irreverent McCafferty brothers were extremely popular. And I can see why. I fell in love with each of these men who were tough, rugged, and dedicated to their family and strong Montana ranching roots.

In each of the books one McCafferty brother discovers true love while trying to protect his younger sister and solve the mystery surrounding her baby. The series was finally complete with *Best Kept-Lies,*

Randi McCafferty's story. The mystery surrounding the paternity of Randi McCafferty's baby and the danger facing the McCafferty clan is wrapped up in the final book, where, eventually, Randi, too, discovers love everlasting for her and her son.

CEO Thorne McCafferty has returned to Grand Hope, Montana, and the Flying M Ranch intent on taking charge of the situation with his sister. Once he's assured that Randi and her baby are healthy, he plans to cut and run, but that's before he meets beautiful Dr. Nicole Stevenson, a woman he knew as a girl, but barely remembers. For the first time in his life, Thorne's about to lose control.

Rancher Matt McCafferty doesn't believe he could be interested in a professional woman of any kind, least of all a cop. But during the investigation of his sister's hit-and-run accident, he runs into a spitfire of a detective in Kelly Dillinger. Then his mind, his heart, and his life changes.

Maverick Slade McCafferty never expected to run across Jamie Parsons again. The last time he saw her she was a young girl, one who had willingly given him her innocence. Now she's all grown up — a no-nonsense lawyer who won't give him the time of day. Or so she thinks.

Headstrong reporter Randi McCafferty doesn't want, need or accept a bodyguard, but her brothers have hired Kurt Striker to watch her back. Kurt doesn't seem too thrilled with the job, either, but as the danger mounts, the tension and unspoken passion ignite, just as a killer is ready to strike.

I've posted excerpts from the books on my Web site and I even have a new contest and drawing to celebrate The McCaffertys. So, visit me at www.lisajackson.com and sign up. You just might win an autographed Lisa Jackson classic!

I hope you love the McCaffertys as much as I do!

Lisa Jackson

PROLOGUE

"I'm dyin', Randi-girl, and there ain't no two ways about it."

Randi McCafferty stopped short. She'd been hurrying down the stairs, her new boots pinching and ringing on the old wooden steps of the house she'd grown up in — a rambling old ranch house set on a slight rise in the middle of No-Damn-Where, Montana. She'd been thinking of her own situation, hadn't realized her father was half lying in his recliner, staring at the blackened grate of the rock fireplace in the living room. John Randall McCafferty was still a big man, but time had taken its toll on his once commanding stature and had ravaged features that had been too handsome for his own good. "What're you talkin' about?" she asked. "You're going to live forever."

"No one does." He glanced up at her and his eyes held hers. "I just want you to know that I'm leavin' you half the place. The boys, they can fight over the rest of it. The Flying M is gonna be yours. Soon."

"Don't even talk that way," she said, walking into the dark room where the afternoon heat had collected. She glanced through a dusty window, past the porch to the vast acres of the ranch that stretched beneath a wide Montana sky. Cattle and horses grazed in the fields past the stable and barn, moving as restlessly as the wind that made the grass undulate.

"You may as well face it. Come over here. Come on, come on, y'know my bark is worse'n my bite."

"Of course I know it." She'd never seen the bad side of her father's temper, though her half brothers had brought it up time and time again.

"I just want to look at ya. My eyes ain't what they used to be." He chuckled, then coughed so violently his lungs rattled.

"Dad, I think I should call Matt. You should be in a hospital."

"Hell, no." As she crossed the room, he waved a bony hand as if he was swatting a fly. "No damn doctor is gonna do me any good now."

"But —"

"Hush, would ya? For once you listen to

me." Incredibly clear eyes glared up at her. He placed a yellowed envelope in her palm. "This here is the deed. Thorne, Matt and Slade, they own the other half together and that should be interestin'," he said with a morbid chuckle. "They'll probably fight over it like cougars at a kill . . . but don't you worry none. You own the lion's share." He smiled at his own little joke. "You and your baby."

"My what?" She didn't move a muscle.

"My grandson. You're carryin' him, ain't ya?" he asked, his eyes narrowing.

A hot blush burned up the back of her neck. She hadn't told a soul about the baby. No one knew. Except, it seemed, her father.

"You know, I would have rather had you get married before you got pregnant, but that's over and done with and I won't be around long enough to see the boy. But you and he are taken care of. The ranch will see to that."

"I don't need anyone to take care of me."

Her father's smile disappeared. "Sure you do, Randi. Someone needs to look after you."

"I can take care of myself and . . . and a baby. I've got a condo in Seattle, a good job and —"

"And no man. Leastwise none worth his

salt. You gonna name the guy who knocked you up?"

"This conversation is archaic —"

"Every kid deserves to know his pa," the old man said. "Even if the guy's a miserable son of a bitch who left a woman carrying his child."

"If you say so," she replied, her fingers curling over the edge of the envelope. She felt more than paper inside.

As if he guessed her question, he said, "There's a necklace in there, too. A locket. Belonged to your ma."

Randi's throat closed for a second. She remembered the locket, had played with it as a child, reaching for the shiny gold heart with its glittering diamonds as it had hung from her mother's neck. "I remember. You gave it to her on your wedding day."

"Yep." He nodded curtly and his eyes grew soft. "The ring is in there, too. If ya want it."

Her eyes were suddenly damp. "Thanks."

"You can thank me by namin' the son of a bitch who did this to you."

She inched her chin up a notch and frowned.

"You're not gonna tell me, are you?"

Randi looked her father steadily in the eye. McCafferty to McCafferty, she said, "Hell would have to freeze over first."

"Damn it, girl, you're a stubborn thing."

"Guess I inherited it."

"And it'll be your undoin', mark my words."

Randi felt a shadow steal through her heart, a cold premonition that settled deep inside, but she didn't budge. For her unborn child's protection, she sealed her lips.

No one would ever know who fathered her child.

Not even her son.

CHAPTER ONE

"Hell's bells," Kurt Striker grumbled under his breath.

He didn't like the job that was set before him. Not one little bit. But he couldn't say no. And it wasn't just because of the substantial fee attached to the assignment, no, the money was good enough. Tempting. He could use an extra twenty-five grand right now. Who couldn't? A check for half the amount sat on the coffee table. Untouched.

Because of the night before. Because of his secret.

He stood in the living room, a fire crackling and warming the backs of his legs, the sprawling snow-covered acres of the Flying M Ranch visible through frosted windows.

"So, what do you say, Striker?" Thorne McCafferty demanded. The oldest of three brothers, he was a businessman by nature and always took charge. "Have we got a deal? Will you see that our sister is safe?"

The job was complicated. Striker was to become Randi McCafferty's personal body-guard whether she liked it or not. Which she wouldn't. Kurt would lay odds on it. He'd spent enough time with the only daughter of the late John Randall Mc-Cafferty to know that when she made up her mind, it wasn't likely to be changed, not by him, nor by her three half brothers who all seemed to have developed a latent sense of responsibility for their headstrong sibling.

She was trouble. No two ways about it. The way she'd hightailed it out of here only a few hours earlier had clearly indicated her mind was set. She was returning to Seattle. With her child. To her home. To her job. To her old life, and the consequences be damned.

And she was running away.

From her three overbearing half brothers.

And from him.

Striker didn't like the situation one bit, but he couldn't very well confide in these three men, now, could he? As he glanced from one anxious McCafferty brother to the next, he didn't examine his own emotions too closely, didn't want to admit that the reason he was balking at the job was because he didn't want to get tangled up with a woman. Any woman. Especially not with the kid sister of these tough-as-nails, over-protective brothers.

It's a little too late for that now, wouldn't you say?

Randi was a sexy thing. All fire and attitude. A strong woman who would, he suspected, as any self-respecting child of John Randall McCafferty, bulldoze her way through life and do exactly what she wanted to do. She wouldn't like Striker nosing around, prying into her affairs, even if he was trying to insulate her from danger. In fact, she'd probably resent it. Especially now.

"Randi's gonna be ticked." Slade, the youngest McCafferty brother, echoed Striker's thoughts, even though he didn't know the half of it. In jeans and a faded flannel shirt, Slade walked to the window and stared outside at the wintry Montana landscape. Snow covered the fields where a few head of cattle and horses huddled against the cold.

"Of course she'll be ticked. Who wouldn't be?" Matt, brother number two, was seated on the worn leather sofa, the heel of one of his cowboy boots propped onto the coffee table only inches from a check for twelve thousand five hundred dollars. "I'd hate it."

"She doesn't have a choice," Thorne said.

CEO of his own corporation, Thorne was used to giving orders and having his employees obey. He'd recently moved to Grand Hope, Montana, from Denver, but he was still in charge. "We agreed, didn't we?" he was saying as he motioned to his younger brothers. "For her protection and the baby's safety, she needs a bodyguard."

Matt nodded curtly. "Yeah, we agreed. That won't make it any easier for Randi to swallow. Even if Kelly's involved."

Kelly was Matt's wife, an ex-cop who was now a private investigator. She'd agreed to work with Striker, especially on this, her sister-in-law's case. Red-haired and quick-witted, Kelly would be an asset. But Striker wasn't convinced Kelly McCafferty would be the oil on troubled waters as far as Randi was concerned. No — having a relative involved would only make a sticky situation stickier.

He glanced to the window, toward the youngest McCafferty brother. The friend who had dragged him into this mess. But Slade didn't meet his eyes, just continued to stare out the frosty panes.

"Look, we've got to do something and we don't have time to waste. Someone's trying to kill her," Thorne pointed out.

Striker's jaw tightened. This was no joke.

And deep down he knew that he'd take the job; wouldn't trust anyone else to do it. For as bullheaded and stubborn as Randi Mc-Cafferty was, there was something about her, a spark in her brown eyes that seemed to touch him just under the skin, a bit of fire that scorched slightly. It had gotten his attention and hadn't let go.

Last night had been proof enough.

Thorne was agitated, worry evident in the lines of his face, his fingers jangling the keys in his pocket. His stare held Striker's. "Will you take the job, or are we going to have to find someone else?"

The thought of another man getting close to Randi soured Kurt's gut, but before he could respond, Slade finally spoke.

"No one else. We need someone we can trust."

"Amen," Matt agreed, before Slade nodded toward the window where a Jeep was plowing down the lane.

Trust? Jesus!

His teeth clenched so hard they ached.

Slade nodded toward the window where an SUV was steadily approaching. "Looks like Nicole's home."

The tension in Thorne's features softened a bit. Within minutes the front door burst open, and a blast of cold Montana air raced into the room. Dr. Nicole McCafferty, still shaking snow from her coat, crossed the entry as the rumble of tiny feet erupted upstairs and Thorne's two stepdaughters, four-year-old-twins, thundered down the stairs. Laughter and shouts added to the din.

"Mommy! Mommy!" Molly cried, while her shyer sister, Mindy, beamed and threw herself into Nicole's waiting arms.

"Hey, how're my girls?" Nicole asked in greeting, scooping both twins into her arms and kissing them on the cheeks.

"You're coooooold!" Molly said.

Nicole laughed. "So I am."

Thorne, limping slightly from a recent accident, made his way into the entry hall and kissed his wife soundly, the girls wriggling between them.

Striker turned away. Felt he was intruding on an intimate scene. It was the same uncomfortable sensation that had been with him from the get-go when Slade had contacted him about helping out the family, and Kurt had first set foot on the Flying M. It had been in October when Randi McCafferty's car had been forced off the road at Glacier Park. She had gone into premature labor and both she and her new baby had nearly died. She'd been in a coma for a

20

while and when she had awoken she'd struggled with amnesia.

Or so she claimed.

Striker thought the loss of memory, though supported by Randi's doctor, was too convenient. He'd also found evidence that another vehicle had run Randi's rig down a steep hillside, where she'd plowed into a tree. She'd survived, though as she'd recovered and regained her memory, she would say nothing about the accident, or guess who might have been trying to kill her. She'd incriminate no one. Either she didn't know or wouldn't tell. The same was true about the father of her kid. She'd told no one who had sired little Joshua. Kurt scowled at the thought. He didn't want to think of anyone being intimate with Randi, though that was just plain stupid. He had no claim to her; wasn't even certain he liked her.

Then you should have let it go last night . . . you saw her on the landing, watched her take care of her child, then waited until she'd put him to bed . . .

In his mind's eye, Kurt remembered her sitting on the ledge, humming softly, her white nightgown clinging to her body as she cradled her baby and fed him. He'd been upstairs, looking down over the railing and

21

moonlight had spilled over her shoulders, illuminating her like a madonna with child.
The sight had been almost spiritual, but also
sensual, and he'd slowly eased his way into
the shadows and waited. Telling himself he
just wanted to walk down the stairs un-
noticed, one of the floorboards had creaked
and Randi had looked up, seen him there
on the upper landing, his hands over the
railing.

"Come on, let's see what Juanita's got in
the kitchen," Nicole was saying, bringing
Kurt crashing back to the here and now.
"Smells good."

"Cinn-da-mon!" The shyer twin said
while her sister rolled her eyes.

"Cinn-a-mon," Molly corrected.

"We'll find out, won't we?" Nicole shuffled
the girls down the hallway toward the
kitchen while Thorne returned to the living
room.

The smile he'd reserved for his wife and
family had faded and he was all business
again. "So what's it gonna be, Striker? Are
you in?"

"It's a helluva lot of money," Matt reminded him.

"Look, Striker, I'm counting on you."
Slade gave up his position near the window.
Lines of worry pinched the corners of his

eyes. "Someone wants Randi dead. I told Thorne and Matt that if anyone could find out who it was, you could. So are you gonna prove me right or what?"

With only a little bit of guilt he slid the check into the battered leather of his wallet. There wasn't really any point in arguing. There hadn't been from the get-go. Striker could no more let Randi McCafferty take off with her kid and face her would-be killer alone than he could quit breathing.

He planned on nailing the son of a bitch.

Big-time.

"Great!" Randi hadn't gotten more than forty miles out of Grand Hope when her new Jeep started acting weird. The steering was off, and when she pulled to the side of the snow-covered road to survey the damage, she realized that her front left tire was low. And it hadn't been when she'd left. She'd passed a gas station less than a mile back, so she turned her vehicle around, only to discover that the station was closed. Permanently. The door was locked and rusted, a window cracked, the pumps dry.

So far her journey back to civilization wasn't going as planned — not that she'd had much of a plan to begin with. That was the problem. She'd intended to return to

Seattle, of course, and soon, but last night . . . with Kurt . . . oh, hell. She'd gotten up this morning and decided she couldn't wait another minute.

All of her brothers were now married. She was, once again, the odd woman out, and she was the reason that they were all in danger. She had to do something about it.

But you're kidding yourself, aren't you? The real reason you left so quickly has nothing to do with your brothers or the danger, and everything to do with Kurt Striker.

She glanced in the rearview mirror, saw the pain in her eyes and let out her breath. She was no good at this, and had never wanted to play the martyr.

"Get on with it," she muttered. She'd just have to change the damn tire herself. Which should be no problem. She'd learned a lot about machinery growing up on the Flying M. A flat tire was a piece of cake. The good news was that she was off the road and relatively dry and protected from the wind under the overhang of the old garage.

With her baby asleep in his car seat, she pulled out the jack and spare, then got to work. Changing the tire wasn't hard, just tedious, and her gloves made working with the lug nuts a challenge. She found the problem with the tire: somewhere she'd picked up a long nail, which had created the slow leak.

It crossed her mind that maybe the flat wasn't an accident, that perhaps the same creep who had forced her off the road at Glacier Park, then attempted to kill her again in the hospital, and later burned the stable might be back to his old tricks. She straightened, still holding the tire iron.

Bitterly cold, the wind swept down the roadway, blowing the snow and lifting her hair from her face. She felt a frisson of fear slide down her spine as she squinted, her gaze sweeping the harsh, barren landscape.

But she saw no one.

Heard nothing.

Decided she was just becoming paranoid.

Which was a really bad thought.

Huddled against the rain, the intruder slid a key into the lock of the dead bolt, then with surprising ease broke into Randi McCafferty's Lake Washington home.

The area was upscale, and the condo worth a fortune. Of course. Because the princess would have no less.

Inside, the unit was a little cluttered. Not too bad, but certainly not neat as a pin. And it had suffered from neglect in the past few months. Dust had settled on the surface of a small desk pushed into the corner, cob-webs floated from a high ceiling, and dust bunnies had collected in the corners. Three-month-old magazines were strewn over a couple of end tables and the meager con-tents of the refrigerator had spoiled weeks ago. Framed prints and pictures splashed color onto warm-toned walls, and an eclec-tic blend of modern and antique furniture was scattered around the blackened stones of a fireplace where the ashes were cold.

Randi McCafferty hadn't been home for a long, long time.

But she was on her way.

Noiselessly, the intruder stalked through the darkened rooms, down a short hallway to a large master suite with its sunken tub, walk-in closet and king-size bed. There was another bath, as well, and a nursery, not quite set up but ready for the next little Mc-Cafferty. The bastard.

Back in the living room there was a desk and upon it a picture, taken years ago, of the three McCafferty brothers — tall, strap-ping, cocky, young men with smiles that could melt a woman's heart and tempers that had landed them in too many barroom brawls to count. In the snapshot they were astride horses. In front of the mounted men, in bare feet, cutoff jeans, a sleeveless shirt and ratty braids, was Randi. She was squinting hard, her head tilted, one hand over her eyes to shade them, that same arm obviously scraped. Twined in the fingers of her other hand she held the reins of all three horses, as if she'd known then that she would lead her brothers around for the rest of their lives.

The bitch.

Disturbed, the intruder looked away from the framed photograph, quickly pushed the play button on the telephone answering machine and felt an instant of satisfaction at having the upper hand on the princess. But the feeling was fleeting. As cold as the ashes in the grate.

As the single message played, resounding through the vaulted room, it became evident that there was only one thing that would make things right.

Randi McCafferty had to pay.

And she had to pay with her life.

CHAPTER TWO

Less than two hours after his conversation with the McCafferty brothers, Striker was aboard a private plane headed due west. A friend who owned this prop job owed him a favor and Striker had called in his marker. He'd also taken the time to phone an associate who was already digging into Randi's past. Eric Brown was ex-military, and had spent some time with the FBI before recently going out on his own. While Striker was watching Randi, Brown would track down the truth like a bloodhound on the trail of a wounded buck. It was just a matter of time.

Staring out the window at the thick clouds, listening to the steady rumble of the engines, Striker thought about Randi McCafferty.

Beautiful. Smart. Sexy as hell.

Who would want her dead?

And why?

Because of the kid? Nah . . . that didn't wash. The book she'd been writing? Or something else, some other secret she'd kept from her brothers.

She was an intriguing, sharp-tongued woman with fire in her brown eyes and a lightning-quick sense of humor that kept even her three half brothers at bay. True, Thorne, Matt and Slade could have held a grudge. All three of them had ended up sharing half the ranch while she, John McCafferty's only daughter, had inherited the other half. Though some of the towns-people of Grand Hope thought differently, Striker knew that the brothers were clean, their motives pure. Hadn't they hired him for the express purpose of saving their half sister's lovely hide? No, they were out as suspects. They weren't trying to murder her.

Chewing on a toothpick, he frowned into the clouds that were visible through the window. Most murders were committed because of greed, jealousy or revenge. Sometimes a victim was killed because they posed a threat, had something over on the killer. Once in a while someone was mur-dered to cover up other crimes.

So why would someone want to kill Randi? Because of her inheritance? Because of her son? A love affair gone sour? Had she swindled someone out of something? Did she know too much? Unconnected motives rattled through his brain. He scratched the side of his face.

There were two mysteries surrounding Randi. The first was the paternity of her child, a closely guarded secret. The second was about a book she'd been writing around the time of the accident.

None of her brothers, nor anyone close to her, professed to know who had sired the baby, probably not even the father. Randi had been tight-lipped on the subject. Striker wondered if she was protecting the father or just didn't want him to know. He thought it wouldn't be too hard to figure out who was little Joshua's daddy. Striker had already found out the kid's blood type from the hospital and he'd managed to get a few hairs from Joshua's head . . . just in case he needed a DNA match.

There were three men who had been close to Randi, close enough to be lovers, though he, as yet, had not substantiated which — if any — she had been intimate with. At that thought his gut clenched. He felt a jolt of jealousy. Ridiculous. He wouldn't allow himself to get emotionally involved with Randi McCafferty, not even after last night. She was his client, even though she didn't know it yet. And when she found out, he was certain the gates of hell would spring open and all sorts of demons would rise up. No, Randi McCafferty wouldn't take kindly to her brothers' safeguards for her.

He tapped his finger on the cold glass of the plane's window and wondered who had warmed Randi's bed and fathered her son.

Bile rose in his throat as he thought of the prime candidates.

Sam Donahue, the ex-rodeo rider, was at the top of the list. Kurt didn't trust the rugged cowboy who had collected more women than pairs of boots. Sam had always been a rogue, a man none of Randi's brothers could stomach, a jerk who had already left two ex-wives in his dusty wake.

Joe Paterno was a freelance photographer who sometimes worked for the *Seattle Clarion.* Joe was a playboy of the worst order, a love-'em-and-leave-'em type who'd been connected to women all over the planet, especially in the political hot spots he photographed. Joe would never be the kind to settle down with a wife and son.

Brodie Clanton, a shark of a Seattle lawyer who'd been born with a silver spoon firmly wedged between his teeth, was the grandson of Judge Nelson Clanton, one of Seattle's most prestigious lawmakers. Brodie Clanton looked upon life as if it owed him something, and spent most of his time defending rich clients.

Not exactly a sterling group to choose from.

What the hell had Randi been thinking? None of these guys was worth her looking at a second time. And yet she'd been linked to each of them. For a woman who wrote a column for singles, she had a lousy track record with men.

And what about you? Where do you fit in?

"Damn." Striker wouldn't think about that now. Wouldn't let last night cloud his judgment. Even if he found out who was the father of the baby, that was just a start. It only proved Randi had slept with the guy. It didn't mean that he was trying to kill her.

Anyone might be out to get Randi. A jealous coworker, someone she'd wronged, a nutcase who had a fixation on her, an old rival, any damn one. The motive for getting her out of the way could include greed or jealousy or fear . . . at this point no one knew. He shifted his toothpick from one side of his mouth to the other and listened as the engines changed speed and the little plane began its descent to a small airstrip south of Tacoma.

The fun was just about to begin.

■ ■ ■ ■

Rain spat from the sky. Bounced on the hood of her new Jeep. Washed the hilly streets of Seattle from a leaden sky. Randi McCafferty punched the accelerator, took a corner too quickly and heard her tires protest over the sound of light jazz emanating from the speakers. It had been a hellish drive from Montana, the winter weather worse than she'd expected, her nerves on edge by the time she reached the city she'd made her home. A headache was building behind her eyes, reminding her that it hadn't been too many months since the accident that had nearly taken her life and robbed her of her memory for a while. She caught a glimpse of her reflection in the rearview mirror — at least her hair was growing back. Her head had been shaved for the surgery and now her red-brown hair was nearly two inches long. For a second she longed to be back in Grand Hope with her half brothers.

She flipped on her blinker and switched lanes by rote, then eased to a stop at the next red light. Much as she wanted to, she couldn't hide out forever. It was time to take action. Reclaim her life. Which was here in

Seattle, not at the Flying M Ranch in Montana with her three bossy half brothers.

And yet her heart twisted and she felt a moment's panic. She'd let herself become complacent in the safety of the ranch, with three strong brothers ensuring she and her infant son were secure.

No more.

You did this, Randi. It's your fault your family is in danger. And now you've compounded the problem with Kurt Striker. What's wrong with you? Last night . . . remember last night? You caught him watching you on the ledge, knew that he'd been staring, had felt the heat between the two of you for weeks, and what did you do? Did you pull on your robe and duck into your bedroom and lock the door like a sane woman? Oh, no. You put your baby down in his crib and then you followed Striker, caught up with him and —

A horn blasted from behind her and she realized the light had turned green. Gritting her teeth, she drove like a madwoman. Pushed the wayward, erotic thoughts of Kurt Striker to the back of her mind for the time being. She had more important issues to deal with.

At least her son was safe. If only for the time being. She missed him horridly already and she'd just dropped him off at a spot where no one could find him. It was only until she did what she had to do. Hiding Joshua was best. For her. For him. For a while. A short while, she reminded herself. Already attempts had been made upon her life and upon the lives of those closest to her, she couldn't take a chance with her baby.

As she braked for a red light, she stared through the raindrops zigzagging down the windshield, but in her mind's eye she saw her infant son with his inquisitive blue eyes, shock of reddish-blond hair and rosy cheeks. She imagined his soft little giggles. So innocent. So trusting.

Her heart tore and she blinked back a sudden spate of hot tears that burned her eyelids and threatened to fall. She didn't have time for any sentimentality. Not now.

The light changed. She eased into the traffic heading toward Lake Washington, weaving her way through the red taillights, checking her rearview mirror, assuring herself she wasn't being followed.

You really are paranoid, her mind taunted as she found the turnoff to her condominium and the cold January wind buffeted the trees surrounding the short lane. But then she had a right to be. She pulled into her parking spot and cranked off the ignition of her SUV. The vehicle was new, a replacement for her crumpled Jeep that had been forced off the road in Glacier Park a couple of months back. The culprit who'd tried to kill her had gotten away with his crime.

But not for long, she told herself as she swung out of the vehicle and grabbed her bag from the back seat. She had work to do; serious work. She glanced over her shoulder one last time. No shadowy figure appeared to be following her, no footsteps echoed behind her as she dashed around the puddles collecting on the asphalt path leading to her front door.

Get a grip. She climbed the two steps, juggled her bag and purse on the porch, inserted her key and shoved hard on the door with her shoulder.

Inside, the rooms smelled musty and unused. A dead fern in the foyer was shedding dry fronds all over the hardwood floor. Dust covered the windowsill.

It sure didn't feel like home. Not anymore. But then nowhere did without her son. She kicked the door behind her and took two steps into the living room, then, seeing a shadow move on the couch, stopped dead in her tracks.

Adrenaline spurted through her blood-stream.

Goose bumps rose on the back of her arms.

Oh, God, she thought wildly, her mouth dry as a desert.

The killer was waiting for her.

CHAPTER THREE

"Well, well, well," he drawled slowly. "Look who's finally come home."

In an instant Randi recognized his voice.

Bastard.

His hand reached to the table lamp. As he snapped on the lights, she found herself staring into the intense, suspicious gaze of Kurt Striker, the private investigator her brothers had seen fit to hire.

She instantly bristled. Fear gave way to outrage. "What the hell are you doing here?"

"Waitin'."

"For?"

"You."

Damn, his drawl was irritating. So was the superior, know-it-all attitude that emanated from him as he lounged on her chenille couch, the fingers of one big hand wrapped possessively around a long-necked bottle of beer. He appeared as out of place in his jeans, cowboy boots and denim jacket as a cougar at a pedigreed-cat show.

"Why?" she demanded as she dropped her bag and purse on a parson's table in the entry. She didn't step into the living room; didn't want to get too close to this man. He bothered her. Big-time. Had from the first time she'd laid eyes on him when she'd still been recuperating from the accident.

Striker was a hardheaded, square-jawed type who looked like Hollywood's version of a rogue cop. His hair, blond streaked, was unruly and fell over his eyes, and he seemed to have avoided getting close to a razor for several days. Deep-set, intelligent eyes, poised over chiseled cheeks, were guarded by thick eyebrows and straight lashes. He wore faded jeans, a tattered Levi's jacket and an attitude that wouldn't quit.

Resting on the small of his back, sprawled on her couch, he raked his gaze up her body one slow inch at a time.

"I asked you a question."

"I'm trying to save your neck."

"You're trespassing."

"So call the cops."

"Enough with the attitude." She walked to the windows, snapped open the blinds. Through the wet glass she caught a glimpse of the lake, choppy, steel-colored water sporting whitecaps and fog too dense to see the opposite shore. Folding her arms over her chest, she turned and faced Striker again.

He smiled then. A dazzling, sexy grin offset by the mockery in his green eyes. It damn near took her breath away and for a splintered second she thought of the hours they'd spent together, the touch of his skin, the feel of his hands . . . oh, God. If he wasn't such a pain in the butt, he might be considered handsome. Interesting. Sexy. Long legs shoved into cowboy boots, shoulders wide enough to stretch the seams of his jacket, flat belly . . . Yeah, all the pieces fit into a hunky package. If a woman was looking for a man. Randi wasn't. She'd learned her lesson. Last night was just a slip. It wouldn't happen again.

Couldn't.

"You know," he said, "I was just thinkin' the same thing. Let's both shove the attitudes back where they came from and get to work."

"To work?" she asked, rankled. She needed him out of her condo and fast. He had a way of destroying her equilibrium, of setting her teeth on edge.

"That's right. Cut the bull and get down to business."

"I don't think we have any business."

His eyes held hers for a fraction of a second and she knew in that splintered instant that he was remembering last night as clearly as she. He cleared his throat. "Randi, I think we should discuss what happened —"

"Last night?" she asked. "Not now, okay? Maybe not ever. Let's just forget it."

"Can you?"

"I don't know, but I'm sure as hell going to try."

He silently called her a liar.

"Okay, if this is the way you want to play it."

"I told you we don't have any business."

"Sure we do. You can start by telling me who's the father of your baby."

Never, buddy. Not a chance. "I don't think that's relevant."

"Like hell, Randi." He was on his feet in an instant, across the hardwood floor and glaring down his crooked nose at her. "There have been two attempts on your life. One was the accident, and I use the term loosely, up in Glacier Park, when your car was forced off the road. The other when someone tried to do you in at the hospital. You remember those two little incidents, don't you?"

She swallowed hard. Didn't answer.

"And let's not forget the fire in the stable at the ranch. Arson, Randi. Remember? It nearly killed your brothers." Her heart squeezed at the painful memory. To her surprise he grabbed her, strong hands curling around her upper arms and gripping tightly through her jacket. "Do you really want to take any more chances with your life? With your brothers'? With your kid's? Little J.R. nearly died from an infection in the hospital after the accident, didn't he? You went into labor early in the middle of no-goddamn-where, and by the time some Good Samaritan saw you and called for an ambulance, your baby almost didn't make it."

She fought the urge to break down. Wished to heaven that he'd quit touching her. He was too close, his angry breath whispering over her face, the raw, sexual energy of him seeping through her clothes.

"Now, I'm not moving," he vowed, "not one bloody inch, until you and I get a few things straight. I'm in for the long haul and I'll stay here all night if I have to. All week. All year."

Her stupid heart pounded, and though she tried to pull away he wouldn't allow it. The manacles surrounding her arms clamped even more tightly.

"Let's start with one important question, shall we?"

He didn't have to ask. She knew what was coming and braced herself.

"Tell me, Randi, right now. No more ducking the issue. Who the devil is J.R.'s father?"

Oh, God, he was too close. "Let go of me," she said, refusing to give in. "And get the hell out of my house."

"No way."

"I'll call the police."

"Be my guest," he encouraged, hitching his chin toward the phone she hadn't used in months. It sat collecting dust on the small desk she'd crammed into one corner of the living room. "Why don't you tell them everything that's happened to you and I'll explain what I'm doing here."

"You weren't invited."

"Your brothers are concerned."

"They can't control me."

He lifted a skeptical eyebrow. "No? They might disagree."

"Big deal," she said, tossing her head and pretending to be tough. The truth was that she loved all of her older half brothers, all three of them, but she couldn't have them poking around in her life. Nor did she

43

want anything to do with Kurt Striker. He was just too damn male for his own good. Or her own. He'd proved that much last night. "Listen, Striker, this is my life. I can handle it. Now, if you'd be so kind as to take your hands off me," she said, sarcasm dripping from the pleasantry, "I have a lot to do."

He stared at her long and hard, those sharp green eyes seeming to penetrate her own. Then he lifted a shoulder and released her. "I can wait."

"Elsewhere."

His smile was pure devilment. "Is that a hint?" he drawled, and again her heart began to trip-hammer. Damn the man.

"A broad one. Take a hike."

"Only if you show me the city."

"What?"

"I'm new in town. Humor me."

"You mean so you can keep an eye on me."

Curse the sexy smile that crawled across his jaw. "That, too."

"Forget it. I've got a million things to do," she said, flipping up a hand to indicate the telephone where no light blinked on her answering machine. "That's odd," she muttered then glanced back at Striker, whom she was beginning to believe was the embodiment of Lucifer. "Wait a minute. You listened to my messages?" she demanded, fury spiking up her spine.

"No, I actually didn't."

She made her way to the desk and pushed the play button on the recorder. "That's odd," she said as she recognized Sarah Peeples's voice.

"Hey, when are you coming back to work?" Sarah asked. "It's soooo boooring with all these A-type males." She giggled. "Well, maybe not that boring, but I miss ya. Give me a call and kiss Joshua for me." The phone clicked as Sarah hung up.

Randi bit her lower lip. Her mind was spinning as she jabbed a finger at the recorder. "You didn't listen to this?"

"No."

"Then who did?"

"Not you?" he asked and his eyes narrowed.

"No, not me." Her skin crawled. If Striker hadn't listened to her messages, then . . . who had? Her headache pounded. Maybe she was jumping at shadows. She was worried about her baby, exasperated with the man in her apartment and just plain tired from the long drive and the few hours' sleep she'd had in the past forty-eight hours. That was it, her nerves were just strung tight. Her brothers hiring this sexy, roughshod P.I. only made things worse. She rubbed her temple and tried to think clearly. "Look, Striker, you can't barge in here, help yourself to a beer, then sit back and make yourself at home . . ."

His expression reminded her that he'd done just that.

"So far," she went on, "I think you've committed half a dozen crimes. Breaking and entering, burglary, trespassing and who knows what else. The police would have a field day."

"So where's your son?" he asked, refusing to be sidetracked. "J.R. Where is he?"

She'd known that was coming. "I call him Joshua."

"Okay, where's Josh?"

"Somewhere safe."

"There is nowhere that's safe."

Her insides crumbled. "You're wrong."

"So you *are* afraid that someone is after you."

"I'm a mother. I'm not taking any chances with him."

"Only with yourself."

"Let's not get into this." She pressed a button and the answering machine rewound.

"Is he with your cousin Nora?"

Her muscles tensed. How had he learned about Nora, on her mother's side? Her brothers had never met Nora.

"Or maybe Aunt Bonita, your mother's stepsister?"

God, he'd done his homework. Her head thundered, her palms suddenly sweaty. "It's none of your business, Striker."

"How about your friend Sharon?" He folded his arms over his chest. "That's where I'm putting my money."

She froze. How could he have guessed that she would leave her precious child with Sharon Okano? She and Sharon hadn't seen each other in nearly nine months, and yet Striker had figured it out.

"You wouldn't take a chance on a relative, or you would have left him in Montana, and your coworkers are out because they might slip up, so it had to be someone you trusted, but not obvious enough that it would be easy to figure it out."

Her heart constricted.

He reached forward and touched her shoulder. She recoiled as if burned.

"If I can guess where you hid him, so can the guy who's after you."

"How did you find Sharon?" she asked. "I'm not buying the 'lucky guess' theory."

Kurt walked to the coffee table and picked

up his beer. "It wasn't rocket science, Randi."

"But —"

"Even cell phones have records."

"You went through my mail to find my phone bill? Isn't that a federal offense, or don't you care about that?" she asked, then her eyes swept the desk and she realized that he couldn't have sorted through the junk mail and correspondence that was hers, as she'd had it held at the post office ages ago.

"It doesn't matter how I got the information," he said. "What's important is that you and your son aren't safe. Your brothers hired me to protect you, and like it or not, that's exactly what I'm going to do." He drained his beer in one long swallow. "Fight me all you want, Randi, but I intend to stick to you like glue. You can call your brothers and complain and they won't budge. You can run away, but I'll catch you so quick it'll make your head spin. You can call the cops and we'll get to the bottom of this here and now. That's just the way it is. So, you can make it easy for everyone and tell me what the hell's going on or you can be difficult and we'll go at it real slow." He set his bottle on one end of the coffee table and as he straightened, his eyes held hers with deadly intensity. "Either way."

"Get out."

"If that's the way you want it. But I'll be back."

So angry she was shaking, she repeated, "Get the hell out."

"You've got one hour to think about it," he advised her as he made his way to the door. "One hour. Then I'll be back. And if we have to, we'll do this the hard way. It's your choice, Randi, but the way I see it, you're damn near out of options."

He walked outside and the door shut behind him. Randi threw the bolt, swore under her breath and fought the urge to crumple into a heap. She forced starch into her spine. Nothing was ever accomplished by falling into a million pieces. It was hard to admit it, but Kurt Striker was right about one thing; she didn't have many choices. Well, that was tough. She wasn't going to be railroaded into making a wrong one.

Too much was at stake.

CHAPTER FOUR

Kurt slid behind the wheel of his rental, a bronze king-cab pickup. The windows were a little fogged, so he cracked one and turned on the defrost to stare through the rivulets of rain sliding down the windshield. He'd give her an hour to sort things out, the same hour he'd give himself to cool off. There was something about the woman that got under his skin and put him on edge.

From the first moment he'd seen her at the Flying M, he'd sensed it — that underlying tension between them, an unacknowledged current that simmered whenever they were in the same room. It was stupid, really. He wasn't one to fall victim to a woman's charms, especially not a spoiled brat of a woman who had grown up as the apple of her father's eye, a rich girl who'd had everything handed to her.

Oh, she was pretty enough. At least she was now that the bruises had disappeared and her hair was growing back. In fact, she was a knockout. Pure and simple. Despite her recent pregnancy, her body was slim, her breasts large enough to make a man notice, her hips round and tight. With her red-brown hair, pointed little chin, pouty lips and wide brown eyes, she didn't need much makeup. Her mind was quick, her tongue rapier sharp and she'd made it more than clear that she wanted him to leave her alone. Which would be best for everyone involved, he knew, but there was just something about her that kept drawing him in and firing his blood.

Forget it. She's your client.

Not technically. She hadn't hired him.

But her brothers had.

You have to keep this relationship professional.

Relationship? What relationship? Hell, she can't stand to be in the same room with me.

Oh, yeah, right. Like you haven't been through this before. And like last night never happened.

She'd put Joshua in his room and then after Kurt had sneaked down the stairway, she'd followed him and found him in the darkened living room where only embers from a dying fire gave off any illumination.

He'd already poured himself a drink and was sipping it quietly while staring through the icy window to the blackened remains of the stable.

"You were watching me," she'd accused, and he'd nodded, not turning around. "Why?"

"I didn't mean to."

"Bull!"

So she wasn't going to let him off the hook. So be it. He took a sip of his drink before facing her.

"What the hell were you doing upstairs?"

"I thought I heard someone, so I checked."

"You did. It was me. This house is full of people, you know." She was so angry, he could feel her heat, noticed that she hadn't bothered buttoning her nightgown, acted as if she was completely unaware that her breasts were visible.

"Do you want me to explain or not?"

"Yeah. Try." She crossed her arms under her breasts, involuntarily lifting them, causing the cleft between them to deepen. Kurt kept his gaze locked with hers.

"As I said, I heard something. Footsteps. I just walked upstairs and down the hall. By the time I started for the stairs you were there."

"And the rest, as they say, is history." She arched an eyebrow and her lips were pursed hard together. "Get a good look?"

"Good enough."

"Like what you saw?"

He couldn't help himself. One side of his mouth lifted. "It was all right."

"What?"

"I've seen better."

"Oh, for the love of St. Jude!" she sputtered, and even in the poor light, he noticed a flush stain her cheeks.

"What did you expect, Randi? You caught me looking, okay? I didn't plan it, but there you were and I was . . . caught. I guess I could have cleared my throat and walked down the stairs, but I was a little . . . surprised." His smile fell away and he took another long swallow. "We're both adults, let's forget it."

"Easy for you to say."

"Not that easy."

Her eyes narrowed up at him. "What's that supposed to mean?"

"You're pretty unforgettable."

"Yeah, right." She ran her fingers through her hair and her nightgown shifted, allowing him even more of a view of her breasts and abdomen. As if finally feeling the breeze, she sucked in her breath and looked

down to see her breasts. "Oh, wonderful."
She fumbled with the buttons. "Here I am
ranting and raving and putting on a show
and . . ."

"It's all right," he said. "I lied before. I've
never seen better."

She shook her head and laughed. "This is
ridiculous."

"Can I buy you a drink?"

"Of my dad's liquor? I don't think so. I
. . . I might do something I'll regret."

"You think?"

She let out a breath, glanced him up and
down and nodded. "Yeah, I think."

He should have stopped himself right then
while he still had a chance of taking control
of the situation, but he didn't and tossed
back his drink. "Maybe regrets are too
highly overrated," he said, dropping his glass
onto a chair and closing the distance between them. He noticed her pulse fluttering
on the smooth skin of her throat, knew that
she was as scared as he was.

But it had been a long time since he'd
kissed a woman and he'd been thinking
about how it would feel to kiss Randi Mc-
Cafferty for weeks. Last night, he'd found
out. He'd wrapped his arms around her and
as a gasp slipped from between her lips, he'd
slanted his mouth over hers and felt his

blood heat. Her arms had instinctively climbed to his shoulders and her body had fitted tight against him.

Warning bells had clanged in his mind, but he'd ignored them as his tongue had slipped between her teeth and his erection had pressed hard against his fly. She was warm and tasted of lingering coffee. His fingers splayed across her back and as she moaned against him, he slowly started inching her nightgown upward, bunching the soft flannel in his fingers as her hemline climbed up her calves and thighs. It seemed the most natural thing in the world to use his weight to carry them both to the rug in front of the dying fire . . .

Now, as he sat in his pickup with the rain beating against his windshield, Striker scowled at the thought of what he'd done. He'd known better than to kiss her, had sensed it wouldn't stop there. He didn't need the complications of a woman.

He hazarded a glance at the third finger of his left hand where he could still see the deep impression a ring had made as it had cut into his skin. The muscles in the back of his neck tightened and a few dark thoughts skated through his mind. Thoughts of another woman . . . another beautiful woman and a little girl . . .

Angry with the turn of his thoughts, he forced his gaze to Randi's condominium. This particular grouping of units rested on a hillside overlooking Lake Washington. He'd parked across the street where he had a clear view of her front door, the only way in or out of the condo, unless she decided to sneak out a window. Even then, he'd see her Jeep leaving. Unless she was traveling on foot, he'd be able to follow her.

He glanced at his watch. She had forty-seven minutes to cool off and get herself together. And so did he. Leaning across the seat, he grabbed his battered briefcase and reached inside where he kept an accordion folder on the McCafferty case. With one eye on the condominium, he riffled through the pages of notes, pictures and columns he'd clipped out of the *Seattle Clarion,* columns with a byline of Randi McCafferty and accompanied by a smiling picture of the author.

"Solo," by Randi McCafferty.

Hers was an advice column for singles, from the confirmed bachelors to the newly divorced, the recently widowed or anyone else who wrote in, claimed not to be married and asked for her opinion. Striker reread a few of his favorites. In one, she advised a woman suffering from abuse to leave the relationship immediately and file charges. In another she told an overly protective single mother to give her teenage daughter "breathing space" while keeping in touch. In still another, she suggested a widower join a grief-support group and take up ballroom dancing, something he and his wife had always wanted to do. Her columns were often empathetic, but sometimes caustic. She told one woman who couldn't decide between two men and was lying to them both to "grow up," while she advised another young single to "quit whining" about his new girlfriend, who sometimes parked in "his" spot while staying over. Within each bit of advice, Randi often added a little humor. It was no wonder the column had been syndicated and picked up in other markets.

Yet there were rumors of trouble at the *Clarion.* Randi McCafferty and her editor, Bill Withers, were supposedly feuding. Striker hadn't figured out why. Yet. But he would. Randi had also written some articles for magazines under the name of R. J. McKay. Then there was her unfinished tell-all book on the rodeo circuit, one she wouldn't talk much about. A lot going on with Ms. McCafferty. Yep, he thought, leaning back and staring at the front door of her place, she was an interesting woman, and one definitely off-limits.

Well, hell, weren't they all? He scowled through the raindrops zigzagging down his windshield and his thoughts started to wend into that forbidden territory of his past, to a time that now seemed eons ago, before he'd become jaded. Before he'd lost his faith in women. In marriage. In life. A time he didn't want to think about. Not now. Not ever.

"He's okay?" Randi said into her cell phone. Her hands were sweaty, her mind pounding with fear, and it was all she could do to try to calm her rising sense of panic. Despite her bravado and in-your-face attitude with Striker, she was shaky. Nervous. His warnings putting her on edge, and now, as she held the cell phone to her ear and peered through the blinds to the parking lot where Kurt Striker's old pickup was parked, her heart was knocking.

"You dropped him off less than an hour ago," Sharon assured her. "Joshua's just fine. I fed him, changed him and put him down for a nap. Right now he's sleeping like a . . . well, a baby."

Randi let out her breath, ran a shaking hand over her lip. "Good."

"You've got to relax. I know you're a new mother and all, but believe me, whatever you're caught up in, stressing out isn't going to help anyone. Not you, not the baby. So take a chill pill."

"I wish," Randi said, only slightly relieved.

"Do it . . . Take your own advice. You're always telling people in your column to take a step back, a deep breath and reevaluate the situation. You still belong to the gym, don't you? Take yoga or tae kwon do or kickboxing."

"You think that would do it?"

"Wouldn't hurt."

"Just as long as I know Joshua's safe."

"And sound. Promise." Sharon sighed. "I know you don't want to hear this, but you might consider going out. You know, with a man."

"I don't think so."

"Just because you had a bad experience with one doesn't mean they're all jerks."

"I had a bad experience with more than one."

"Well . . . it wouldn't kill you to give romance a chance."

"I'm not so sure. When Cupid pulls back his bow and aims at me, I swear his arrows are poisoned."

"That's not what you tell the people who

write you."

"With them, I can be objective." She was staring at Striker's truck, which hadn't moved. The man was behind the wheel. She saw movement, but she couldn't see his facial features, could only feel him staring at her house, sizing it up, just as he'd done with her. "Look, I'll be over tomorrow, but if you need to reach me for anything, call me on my cell."

"Will do. Now, quit worrying."

Fat chance, Randi thought as she hung up. Ever since she'd given birth she'd done nothing more than worry. She was worse than her half brothers and that was pretty bad. Thorne was the oldest and definitely type A. But he'd recently married Nicole and settled down with her and her twin girls. Randi smiled at the thought of Mindy and Molly, two dynamic four-year-olds who looked identical but were as different as night and day. Then there was Matt, ex-rodeo rider and serious. Had his own place in Idaho until he'd fallen in love with Kelly, who was now his wife. And then there was Slade. He was a rebel, hadn't grown up worrying about anything. But all of a sudden he'd made it his personal mission to "take care" of his younger, unmarried sister and her child.

A few months ago Randi would have scoffed at her brothers' concerns. But that had been before the accident. She remembered little of it, thank God, but now she had to figure out who was trying to harm her. She could accept Striker's help, she supposed, but was afraid that if she did, if she confided in anyone, she would only be jeopardizing her baby further and that was a chance she wasn't about to take. Regardless of her brothers' concerns.

Frowning, she remembered Matt and Kelly's wedding and the reception afterward. There had been dancing and laughter despite the cold Montana winter, despite the charred remains of the stable, a reminder of the danger she'd brought upon her family. Kelly had been radiant in her sparkling dress, Matt dashing in a black tuxedo, even Slade — who'd been injured in the fire — had forgone his crutches to dance with Jamie Parsons before whisking her away to elope on that snow-covered night. Randi had dressed her son in a tiny tuxedo and held him close, silently vowing to take the danger away from her brothers, to search out the truth herself.

Two days later when a breathless Slade and Jamie had returned as husband and wife, Randi had announced she was leaving.

"Are you out of your ever-lovin' mind?" Matt had demanded. He'd slapped his hat against his thigh and his breath had steamed from his lungs as all four of John Randall McCafferty's children had stood near the burned-out shell of the stable.

"This is beyond insanity." Thorne had glared down at her, as if he could use the same tactics that worked in a boardroom to convince her to stay. "You can't leave."

"Watch me," she'd baited, meeting his harsh gaze with one of her own.

Even Slade, the rebel and her staunchest ally, had turned against her. His crutches buried beyond their rubber tips in a drift of snow at the fence line, he'd said, "Don't do it, Randi. Keep J.R. here with us. Where we can help you."

"This is something I have to do," she'd insisted, and caught a glimpse of Striker, forever lurking in the shadows, always watching her. "I can't stay here. It's unsafe. How many accidents have happened here? Really, it's best if I leave." All of her brothers had argued with her, but Striker had remained silent, not arguing, just taking it all in.

Until last night. And then all hell had broken loose.

So she'd left and he'd followed her to

Seattle. Now she realized she'd have one helluva time getting rid of him. It galled her that her brothers had hired him.

"What makes you think you'll be safer in Seattle than Grand Hope?" Thorne had asked as she'd packed her bags in the pine-walled room she'd grown up in. "You're still not healed completely from the accident. If you stayed here, we could all look after you. And little J.R, er, Joshua, would have Molly and Mindy to play with when he got a little bigger."

Randi's heart was torn. She'd eyed her bright-eyed nieces, Molly bold and impudent, Mindy hiding behind Thorne's pant leg, and known that she couldn't stay. She had things to do; a story to write. And she knew that if she stayed any longer, she'd only get more tangled up with Striker.

"I'll be all right," she'd insisted, zipping up her bag and gathering her baby into her arms. "I wouldn't do anything to put Joshua in danger." As she'd clambered down the stairs, she'd heard the twins asking where she was going and had spied their house-keeper, Juanita, making the sign of the cross over her ample bosom and whispering a prayer in Spanish. As if she would haul her own child into the maw of danger. But they didn't understand that in order for everyone

63

to be safe, she had to get back to her old life and figure out why someone was trying to harm her.

And Joshua. Don't forget your precious son. Whoever it is means business and is desperate. She noted that Striker was still seated in his truck. Waiting. Damn the man. Quickly she closed the blinds, then took a final glance around the small nursery. Hardwood floors that were dusty, a cradle stuck in a corner, a bookcase that was still in its box as "some assembly" was required and she hadn't had time.

Because you were in the hospital.

Because you nearly died.

Because someone is determined to kill you.

Maybe, just maybe, your brothers have a point.

Maybe you should trust Kurt Striker.

Again she thought of the night before. Trust him? Trust herself?

What other choice did she have?

Much as she hated to admit it, he was right. If Kurt could figure out where she'd hidden Joshua, then the would-be killer, whoever he was, could as well. Her insides knotted. Why would anyone want to harm her innocent baby? Why?

It's not about Joshua, Randi. It's about you. Someone wants you dead. As long as the

64

baby isn't with you, he's safe.

She clung to that notion and set about getting her life in order again. She made herself a cup of instant coffee and dialed the office. Her editor was out, but she left a message on his voice mail, checked her own e-mail, then quickly unpacked and changed into a clean sweater, slacks and boots. She wound a scarf around her neck and finger combed her short hair, looking into the hall mirror and cringing. She'd lost weight in the past five months, indeed she now weighed less than before she'd gotten pregnant, and she was having trouble getting used to the length of her hair. She'd always worn it long, but her head had been shaved before one of her lifesaving surgeries to alleviate the swelling in her brain and the resulting grow-out was difficult to adjust to though she'd had it shaped before leaving Montana. Instead, she went into the bathroom, found an old tube of gel and ran some of the goop through her hair. The result was kind of a finger-in-the-light-socket look, but was the best she could do. She was just rinsing her hands when her doorbell buzzed loudly several times, announcing a visitor. She didn't have to be told who was ringing the bell. One quick look at her watch showed her that it had been one hour and five minutes since she'd last faced Striker. Apparently the man was prompt.

And couldn't take a hint.

"Great," she muttered, wiping her hands on a towel and discarding it into an open hamper before hurrying to the front door. What she didn't need was anyone dogging her, bothering her and generally getting in the way. She was a private person by nature and opposed anyone nosing into her business, no matter what his reasons. Reining in her temper, she yanked open the door. Sure as shootin', Kurt Striker, all six feet two inches of pure male determination, was standing on her doorstep. His light brown hair had darkened from the raindrops clinging to it, and his green eyes were hard. Wearing an aging bomber jacket and even older jeans, he was sexy as hell and, from the looks of him, not any happier at being on her stoop than she was to find him there.

"What's with ringing the bell?" she asked, deciding not to mask her irritation. "I thought you had your own key, or a pick, or something. Compliments of my brothers."

"They're only looking out for you."

"They should mind their own business."

"And for your kid."

"I know." She'd already stepped away

from the door and into the living room. Striker was on her heels. She heard the door slam behind him, the lock engage and the sound of his boots ringing on her hardwood floors.

"Look, Randi," he said as she stopped at the closet and found her raincoat. "If I can break in, then —"

"Yeah, yeah, I'm way ahead of you." She slid her arms through the sleeves and glanced up at him. "I'll change the locks, put on a dead bolt, okay?"

"Along with putting in an alarm system and buying a guard dog."

"Hey — I've got a baby. Remember?" She walked to the couch, found her purse and grabbed it. Now . . . the computer. Quickly she tucked her laptop into its case. "I don't think an attack dog would be a good idea."

"Not an attack dog — a guard dog. There's a big difference."

"If you say so. Now, if you'll excuse me, I've got to go to the office." She anticipated what he was about to say. "Look, it wouldn't be a good idea to follow me, you know? I'm already in enough hot water with my boss as it is." She didn't wait for him to answer, just walked back to the door. "So, if you'll excuse me —" She opened the door again in an unspoken invitation.

His lips twisted into a poor imitation of a smile. "You're not going to get rid of me that easily."

"Why? Because of the money?" she asked, surprised that the mention of it bothered her, cut into her soul. "That's what this is all about, isn't it? My brothers have paid you to watch over me, right? You're supposed to be . . . oh, hell . . . not my bodyguard. Tell me Thorne and Matt and Slade aren't so archaic, so controlling, so damn stupid as to think I need a personal bodyguard . . . Oh, God, that's it, isn't it?" She would have laughed if she hadn't been so furious. "This has got to end. I need privacy. I need space. I need —"

His hand snaked out, and fast as lightning, he grabbed her wrist, his fingers a quick, hard manacle. "What you need is to be less selfish," he finished for her. He was so close that she felt his hot, angry breath wafting across her face. "We've been through this before. Quit thinking about your damn independence and consider your kid's safety. Along with your own." He dropped her arm as suddenly as he'd picked it up. "Let's go. I won't get in the way."

The smile he cast over his shoulder was wicked enough to take her breath away. "Promise."

CHAPTER FIVE

"Don't even think about riding with me," she warned, flipping the hood of her jacket over her hair as she dashed toward her Jeep. The rain had softened to a thick drizzle, a kind of mist that made visibility next to nil. It was early evening, the sky dark with heavy clouds.

"It would make things a helluva lot easier."

Obviously, Striker wasn't taking a hint. Collar turned up, he kept with her as she reached the car.

"For whom?" She shot him a look and clicked on her keyless remote. The Jeep beeped and its interior lights flicked on.

"Both of us."

"I don't think so." She climbed into her car and immediately locked her doors. He didn't move. Just stood by the Jeep. As if she would change her mind. She switched on the ignition as she tossed off her hood. Then, leaving Striker standing in the rain, she backed out of her parking spot, threw the Jeep into Drive and cruised out of the lot. In the rearview mirror, she caught a glimpse of him running toward his truck, but not before she managed to merge into the traffic heading toward the heart of the city. She couldn't help but glance in her mirrors, checking to see if Striker had followed.

Not that she doubted it for a minute. But she didn't see his truck and reminded herself to pay attention to traffic and the red taillights glowing through the rain. She couldn't let her mind wander to the man, not even if she had acted like a fool last night.

She'd let him kiss her, let him slide her nightgown off her body, felt his lips, hot and hard, against the hollow of her throat and the slope of her shoulder. She shouldn't have done it, known it was a mistake, but her body had been a traitor and as his rough fingers had scaled her ribs and his beard-rough face had rubbed her skin, she'd let herself go, kissed him feverishly.

She'd been surprised at how much she'd wanted him, how passionately she'd kissed him, scraped off his clothes, ran her own anxious fingers down his hard, sinewy shoulders to catch in his thick chest hair.

The fire had hissed quietly, red embers glowing, illuminating the room to a warm orange. Her breathing had been furious, her heart rocketing, desire curling deep inside her. She'd wanted him to touch her, shivered when his tongue brushed her nipples, bitten her bottom lip as his hot breath had caressed her abdomen and legs. She'd opened to him easily as his hands had explored and touched. Her mind had spun in utter abandon and she'd wanted him . . . Oh, God, she'd wanted him as she'd never wanted another man.

Which had been foolish . . . but as he'd kissed her intimately and slid the length of his body against her, she'd lost all control. All her hard-fought willpower . . .

She nearly missed her exit as she thought about him and the magic of the night, the lovemaking that had caused her to steal away early in the morning, before dawn. As if she'd been ashamed.

Now she wended her way off I-5 and down the steep streets leading to the waterfront. Through the tall, rain-drenched buildings was a view of the gray waters of Eliot Bay — restless and dark, mirroring her own uneasy feelings. She pulled the Jeep into the newspaper's parking lot, grabbed her laptop and briefcase and faced a life that she'd left months before.

The offices of the *Seattle Clarion* were housed on the fifth floor of what had originally been a hotel. The hundred-year-old building was faced in red brick and had been updated, renovated and cut into offices.

Inside, Randi punched the elevator button. She was alone, rainwater dripping from her jacket as the ancient car clamored upward. It stopped twice, picking up passengers before landing on the fifth floor, the doors opening to a short hallway and the etched-glass doors of the newspaper offices. Shawn-Tay, the receptionist, looked up and nearly came unglued when she recognized Randi.

"For the love of God, look at you!" she said, shooting to her feet and disconnecting her headset in one swift movement. Model tall, with bronze skin and dark eyes, she whipped around her desk and hugged Randi as if she'd never stop. "What the devil's got into you? Never callin' in. I was worried sick about you. Heard about the accident and . . ." She held Randi at arm's length. "Where's that baby of yours? How dare you come in here without him?" She cocked her head at an angle. "The hair works, but you've lost too much weight."

"I'll work on that."

"Now, about the baby?" Shawn-Tay's eyebrows elevated as the phone began to ring. "Oh, damn. I gotta get that, but you come back up here and tell me what the hell's been going on with you." She rounded the desk again and slid lithely into her chair. Holding the headset to one ear, she said, "*Seattle Clarion,* how may I direct your call?"

Randi slid past the reception desk and through the cubicles and desks of co-workers. Her niche was tucked into a corner, in the news section, behind a glass wall that separated the reporters from the salespeople. In the time she'd been gone, the walls had been painted, from a dirty off-white to different shades at every corner. Soft purple on one wall, sage on another, gold or orange on the next, all tied together by a bold carpet mingling all the colors. She passed by several reporters working on deadlines, though much of the staff had gone home for the day. A few night reporters were trickling in and the production crew still had hours to log in, but all in all, the office was quiet.

She slid into her space, surprised that it was just as she'd left it, that the small cubicle hadn't been appropriated by someone else, as it had been months since she'd been in Seattle or sat at her desk. She'd set up maternity leave with her boss late last summer and she'd created a cache of columns in anticipation of taking some time off to be with the baby and finishing the book she'd started. Between those new columns and culling some older ones, hardly vintage, but favorites, there had been enough material to keep "Solo" in the Living section twice a week, just like clockwork.

But it was time to tackle some new questions, and she spent the next two hours reading the mail that had stacked up in her in box and skimming the e-mails she hadn't collected in Montana. As she worked, she was vaguely aware of the soft piped-in music that sifted through the offices of the *Clarion,* and the chirp of cell phones in counterpoint to the ringing of land lines to the office. Conversation, muted and seemingly far away, barely teased her ears.

In the back of her mind she wondered if Kurt Striker had followed her. If, even now, he was making small talk with Shawn-Tay in the reception area. The thought brought a bit of a smile to her lips. Striker wasn't the type for small talk. No way. No how. For the most part tight-lipped, he was a sexy man whose past was murky, never discussed. She had the feeling that at one point in his life, he'd been attached to some kind of police department; she didn't know where or why he was no longer a law officer. But she'd find out. There were advantages to working for a newspaper and one of them was access to reams of information. If he wasn't forthcoming on his own, she'd do some digging. It wouldn't be the first time.

"Hey, Randi!" Sarah Peeples, movie reviewer for the *Clarion,* was hurrying toward Randi's desk. Sarah's column, "What's Reel," was published each Friday and was promoted as "hip and happening." A tall woman with oversize features, a wild mop of blond curls and a penchant for expensive boots and cheap jewelry, Sarah spent hours watching movies in theaters, on DVDs and tapes. She lived and breathed movies, celebrities and all things Hollywood. Today she was wearing a choker that looked as if it had been tailored for a rottweiler or a dominatrix, boots with pointed toes and silver studs, a gray scoop-necked sweater and a black skirt that opened in the front, slitted high enough to show off just a flash of thigh. "I was beginning to think I might never see you again."

"Can't keep a good woman down," Randi quipped.

"Amen. Where the hell have you been?"

"Montana with my brothers."

"The hair is new."

"Necessity rather than fashion."

"But it works for you. Short and sassy." Sarah was bobbing her head up and down as if agreeing with herself. "And you look great. How's the baby?"

"Perfect."

"And when will I get to meet him?"

"Soon," Randi hedged. The less she spoke about Joshua, the better. "How're things around here?"

Sarah rolled her eyes as she rested a hip on Randi's desk. "Same old, same old. I've been bustin' my butt . . . well, if you can call it that, rereviewing all the movies that are Oscar contenders."

"Sounds exhausting," Randi drawled.

"Okay, so it's not digging ditches, I know, but it's work."

"Has anything strange been going on around here?" Randi asked.

"What do you mean? Everyone who works here is slightly off, right?"

"I guess you're right."

Sarah picked up a glass paperweight and fiddled with it. "Now, when are you going to bring the baby into the office and show him off?" Sarah's grin was wide, her interest sincere. She'd been married three years and desperately wanted a baby. Her husband was holding out for the big promotion that would make a child affordable. Randi figured it might never come.

"When things have calmed down." She considered confiding in Sarah, but thought better of it. "He and I need to get settled in."

"Mmm. Then how about pictures?"

"I've got a ton of 'em back at the condo. Still packed. I'll bring them next time, I promise," she said, then leaned back in her chair. "So fill me in. What's going on around here?"

Sarah was only too glad to oblige. She offered up everything from office politics, to management changes, to out-and-out gossip. In return, she wanted to know every detail of Randi's life in Montana, starting with the accident. Finally, she said, "Paterno's back in town."

Randi felt the muscles in her back grow taut. "Is he?" Forty-five, twice divorced with a hound-dog face, thick hair beginning to gray and a razor-sharp sense of humor, the freelance photographer had asked Randi out a few years back and they'd dated for a while. It hadn't worked out for a lot of reasons. The main reason being that, at the time, neither one of them had wanted to commit. Nor had they been in love.

"He's been asking about you." Sarah set the paperweight onto the desk again. "You know, unless you're involved with someone, you might want to give him another chance."

Randi shook her head. "I don't think so."

"You hiding something from him?"

"What?" Randi asked, searching her friend's face. "Hiding something? Of course not . . . Oh, I get it." She shook her head and sighed. No one knew the identity of her son's father; not even the man himself. Before she could explain, Sarah's cell phone beeped.

"Oops. Duty calls," Sarah said, eyeing the face of the phone as a text message appeared. "New films just arrived. Well, old ones really. I'm doing a classic film noir piece next month and I ordered a bunch of old Peter Lorre, Bette Davis and Alfred Hitchcock tapes to review." She cast a smile over her shoulder as she hurried off. "Guess what I'll be doing this weekend? Drop by if you don't have anything better to do. . . ."

"Yeah, yeah, I know. I won't hold my breath."

Good thing, Randi thought, as she didn't seem to have a moment to breathe. She had way too much to do, she thought as she turned on her computer.

And the first item on her agenda was finding a way to deal with Kurt Striker.

". . . that's right. All three of 'em are back in Seattle," Eric Brown was saying, his voice crackling from his cell phone's connection to that of Striker's. "What're the chances of that? Clanton lives here but the other two don't. Paterno, he's at least got a place here, but Donahue doesn't."

Striker didn't like it.

"Paterno arrived three days ago and Donahue rolled into town yesterday."

Just hours before Randi had returned. "Coincidence?" Striker muttered, not believing it for a second as he stood on the sidewalk outside the offices of the *Clarion.*

There was a bitter laugh on the other end of the line. "If you believe that, I've got some real estate in the Mojave —"

"— that you want to sell me. Yeah, I know," Striker growled angrily. "Clanton lives here. Paterno does business in town. But Donahue . . ." His jaw tightened. "Can you follow him?"

"Not if you want me to stick around and watch the condo."

Damn it all. There wasn't enough manpower for this. Striker and Brown couldn't be in three places at once. "Just stay put for now. But let me know if anything looks odd to you, anything the least bit suspicious."

"Got it, but what about the other two guys? Paterno and Clanton?"

"Check 'em out, see what they're up to, but it's Donahue who concerns me most. We'll talk later." Striker hung up, then called Kelly McCafferty and left a message when she didn't answer. Angry at the world, he snapped his phone shut. All three of the men with whom Randi had been involved were here. In the city. Great . . . Just . . . great. His shoulders were bunched against the cold, his collar turned up and inside he felt a knot of jealousy tightening in his gut.

Jealousy, and even envy for that matter, were emotions Striker detested, the kind of useless feelings he'd avoided, even while he'd been married. Maybe that had been the problem. Maybe if he'd felt a little more raw passion, a little more jealousy or anger or empathy during those first few years of marriage, shown his wife that he'd cared about her, maybe then things would have turned out differently . . . Oh, hell, what was he thinking? He couldn't change the past. And *the accident,* that's how they'd referred to it, *the accident* had altered everything, created a deep, soul-wrenching, damning void that could never be filled.

And yet last night, when he'd been with Randi . . . Touched her. Kissed her. Felt her warmth surround him, he'd felt differently. *Don't make too much of it. So you made love to her. So what?* Maybe it had just been so long since he'd been with a woman that last night seemed more important than it was.

Whatever the reason, he couldn't stop thinking about it. Couldn't forget how right it had felt.

And it had been so wrong.

In an effort to dislodge images of Randi lying naked in front of the fire, staring up at him with those warm eyes, Striker bought coffee from a vendor and resumed his position not far from the door, protected by the awning of an antique bookstore located next door to the *Clarion*'s offices.

A familiar ache, one he rarely acknowledged, tore through him as he sipped his coffee. Leaning a shoulder against the rough bricks surrounding plate-glass windows etched in gold-leaf lettering, he watched the door of the *Clarion*'s building through a thin wisp of steam rising from his paper cup. Pedestrians scurried past in trench coats, parkas or sweatshirts, some wearing hats, a few with umbrellas, most bareheaded, their collars turned to the wind and rain that steadily dripped from the edge of the awning.

His cell phone rang and he swung it from his pocket. "Striker."

"Hi, it's Kelly."

For the first time in hours, he smiled as Matt's wife started rattling off information. The men at the Flying M were still upset about Randi's leaving. Kelly was working to find a maroon Ford, one that was scraped up and dented from pushing Randi's vehicle off the road in Glacier Park. Kelly was also double-checking all of the staff who had been on duty the night that Randi was nearly killed in the hospital. So far she'd come up with nothing.

Striker wasn't surprised.

He hung up knowing nothing more than when he'd taken the call. Whoever was trying to kill Randi was either very smart or damn lucky.

So far.

Cars, vans and trucks, their windows fogged, sped through the old, narrow streets of this part of the city. Striker glared at the doorway of the hotel, drank coffee and scowled as he considered the other men in Randi McCafferty's life, at least one of whom had bedded her and fathered her son.

Paterno. Clanton. Donahue. Bastards

every one of them.

But he was narrowing the field. He'd done some double-checking on the men who had been involved with Randi. It was unlikely that Joe Paterno had fathered the kid. The timing was all wrong. Kurt had looked into Paterno's travel schedule and records. Paterno had been in Afghanistan around the time the baby had been conceived. There had been rumors that he'd been back in town for a weekend, but Kurt had nearly ruled out the possibility by making a few phone calls to Paterno's chatty landlady. Unless Paterno hadn't shown his face at his apartment and holed up for a secret weekend alone with Randi, he hadn't fathered the kid. Since Randi had been out of town most of the month, it seemed Joe was in the clear.

Leaving Brodie Clanton, the snake of a lawyer, and Sam Donahue, a rough-around-the-edges cowboy; a man whose shady reputation was as black as his hat. Again jealousy cut through him. Clanton was so damn slick, a rich lawyer and a ladies' man. It galled Striker to think of Randi sleeping with a guy who could barely start a sentence without mentioning that his grandfather had been a judge.

A-number-one jerk if ever there had been

one, Clanton had avoided walking down the aisle so far, the confirmed-bachelor type who was often seen squiring around pseudocelebrities when they blew into town. He was into the stock market, expensive cars and young women, the kind of things a man could trade in easily. Clanton had been in town around the time Joshua had been conceived, but, with a little digging into credit card receipts, Striker had determined that Randi, at that time, had been in and out of Seattle herself. She'd never traveled as far as Afghanistan or, presumably, into Paterno's arms, but she'd been chasing a story with the rodeo circuit, where Sam Donahue was known for breaking broncs and women's hearts.

If Striker had been a betting man, he would have fingered Donahue as the baby's daddy. Twice married, Donahue had cheated on both his wives, leaving number one for a younger woman who'd grown up in Grand Hope, Montana, Randi's hometown. And now he just coincidentally had shown up here. A day before Randi.

Striker's jaw tightened so hard it hurt.

DNA would be the only true answer, of course, unless he forced the truth from Randi's lips. Gorgeous lips. Even when she was angry. Her mouth would twist into a furious pout that Striker found incredibly sexy. Which was just plain nuts. He couldn't, *wouldn't* let his mind wander down that seductively dark path. No matter how attractive Randi McCafferty was, he was being paid to protect her, not seduce her. He couldn't let it happen again.

He felt a bit of hardening beneath his fly and swore under his breath. He shouldn't get an erection just thinking of the woman . . . Hell, this was no time. None whatsoever for ridiculous fantasies. He had a job to do. And he'd better do it quickly before there was another unexplained "accident," before someone else got hurt. Or before the would-be murderer got lucky and this time someone *was* killed.

CHAPTER SIX

She pushed open the revolving glass doors and found him just where she'd expected him, on a rain-washed Seattle street, looking damnably rough-and-tumble and sexy as ever. Obviously waiting for her. Great. Just what she *didn't* need, an invitation to trouble in disreputable jeans and a beat-up jacket.

Yep. Kurt Striker in all his damn-convention attitude was waiting.

Her stupid pulse quickened at the sight of him, but she quickly tamped down any emotional reaction she felt for the man. Yes, he was way too attractive in his tight jeans, leather jacket and rough-hewn features. His face was red with the cold, his hair windblown and damp as he leaned a hip against the bricks of a small shop, his eyes trained on the main door of the building. He was holding a paper cup of coffee, which he tossed into a nearby trash can when he spotted her.

Why did she have a thing for dangerous, sensual types? What was wrong with her? Never once in her life had she been attracted to the boy next door, nor to the affable, respectable, dedicated man who worked nine to five, nor the warm, cuddly football-watching couch potato who would love her to the end of time and never once forget an anniversary. The very men she lauded in her column. The men she advised women to give second glances. The salt-of-the-earth, give-you-the-shirt-off-his-back kind of guy who washed his car and the dog on Saturdays, the guy who wore the same flannel shirt that he'd had since college — the regular Joe of the world. One of the good guys.

Maybe, she thought, crossing the street, that was why she could give out advice to the women and men who were forever falling for the wrong kind. Because she was one of them and, she realized, skirting a puddle as she jaywalked to the parking lot where Striker was posed, she knew the pitfalls of hot-wired attraction. She bore the burn marks and scars to prove it.

"Fancy meeting you here," she said, clicking her Jeep's keyless remote. "You just don't seem to get it, do you? I don't want you here."

"We've been through this."

"And I have a feeling we'll go through it a dozen more times before you get the message." She opened the car door, but he was quick, slamming it shut with the flat of his hand.

"Why don't you and I start over," he suggested, forcing a smile, his arm effectively cutting off her ability to climb into the Jeep. "I'll take you to dinner — there's a nice little Irish pub around the corner — and you can fill me in on your life before you got to Montana."

"There's nothing to tell."

"Like hell." His smile slid away. "It's time you leveled with me. I'm sick to the back teeth of the clamped-lip routine. I need to find out who's been trying to hurt you and your brothers. If you weren't so damn arrogant to think this is just about you, that I'm only digging into all this to bother you, then you'd realize that you're the key to all the trouble that's been happening at the Flying M. It's not just your problem, lady. If you remember, Thorne's plane went down —"

"That was because of bad weather. It was an accident."

"And he was flying in that storm to get

back to Montana because of you and the baby, wasn't he? And what about the fire in the stable? God, woman, Slade nearly lost his life. The fire was ruled arson and it's a little too convenient for me to believe that it was coincidence, okay?"

"Drop it, Striker," she warned, whirling on him.

"No way."

"Why do you think I left the ranch?" she demanded.

"I think you left because of me."

That stopped her short. Standing in the dripping rain with his gaze centered directly on hers, she nearly lost it. "Because of you?"

"And last night."

"Don't flatter yourself."

"The timing is right."

Dear Lord. Her stomach twisted. "Let's get something straight, shall we? I left Montana so that the 'accidents' at the Flying M would stop and my brothers and their families would be safe. Whoever is behind this is after me."

"So you think you're what? Drawing the fire away from your family?"

"Yes."

"What about you? Your kid?"

"I can take care of myself. And my baby."

"Well, you've done a pretty piss-poor job

of it so far," he said, his skin ruddy with the cold, his eyes flashing angrily.

"And you think that confiding in you would help? I don't even know anything about you other than Slade seems to think you're okay."

"You know a helluva lot more than that," he said, and she swallowed against the urge to slap him.

"If you're talking about last night . . ."

"Then what? Go on."

"I can't. Not here. And . . . and besides, that's not the kind of knowing I was talking about. So don't try to bait me, okay?"

His jaw slid to one side and his eyes narrowed. "Fair enough and you're right. You don't know me, but maybe it's time. Let's go. I'll tell you anything you want to know." His grin was about as warm as the Yukon in winter. "I'll buy dinner."

Before she could argue, he grabbed the crook of her arm and propelled her around the corner, down two blocks and toward a staircase that led down a flight to a subterranean bar and restaurant. He helped her to a booth in the back before she finally yanked her arm away. "Where'd you learn your manners? At the Cro-Magnon School of Etiquette?"

"Graduated cum laude." One eyebrow

cocked disarmingly.

She chuckled and bit back another hot retort. Goading him was getting her nowhere fast. But at least he had a sense of humor and could laugh at himself. Besides which, she was starved. Her stomach started making all sorts of vile noises at the smells emanating from the kitchen.

Kurt ordered an ale, and she, deciding a drink wouldn't hurt, did the same. "Okay, okay, so you've made your point," she said when he leaned back in the booth and stared at her. "You take your job seriously. You're not going away. Whatever my brothers are paying you is worth putting up with me and my bad attitude, right?"

He let it slide as the waitress, a reed-thin woman with curly red hair tied into a single plait, reappeared with two frosty glasses, twin dinner menus and a bowl of peanuts. She slid all onto the table, then ambled toward a table where a patron was wagging his finger frantically to get her attention.

The place was dim and decorated with leatherlike cushions, mahogany wood aged to near black, a scarred wooden floor and a ceiling of tooled-metal tiles. It smelled of beer and ale, with the hint of cigar smoke barely noticeable over the tang of food grilling behind the counter. Two men were playing darts in a corner and the click of billiard balls emanated from an archway leading to other rooms. Conversation was light, patrons at the long, battered bar tuned in to a muted Sonics basketball game.

"I'm going to check on the baby." She reached into her bag, retrieved her cell phone and punched out Sharon Okano's number.

Sharon picked up on the second ring and was quick to reassure her that Joshua was fine. He'd already eaten, been bathed and was in his footed jammies, currently fascinated by a mobile Sharon had erected over his playpen.

"I'll be by to see him as soon as I can," Randi said.

"He'll be fine."

"I know. I just can't wait to hold him a minute." Randi clicked off and tried to quell the dull ache that seemed forever with her when she was apart from her child. It was weird, really. Before Joshua's birth she had been free and easy, didn't have a clue what a dramatic change was in store for her. But from the moment she'd awoken from her coma and learned she'd borne a son, she could barely stand to be away from him, even for a few hours.

As for being with him and holding him,

the next few weeks promised to be torture on that score. Until she was certain he was safe with her. She slid the phone into her purse and turned to Kurt, who was studying her intently over the rim of his mug. Great. Dealing with him wasn't going to be easy, either. Even if she didn't factor in that she'd made love to him like a wanton in the wee hours of this very morning.

They ordered. Two baskets of fish and chips complete with sides of coleslaw and a second beer, even though they weren't quite finished with the first, were dropped in front of them.

"Why are you keeping your kid's paternity a secret?" Kurt finally asked. "What does it matter?"

"I prefer he didn't know."

"Why not? Seems as if he has a right."

"Being a sperm donor isn't the same as being a father." Her stomach was screaming for food but the conversation was about to kill her appetite.

"Maybe he should be the judge of that."

"Maybe you should keep your nose in your own business." She took a long swallow from her drink and the guys at the bar gave up a shout as one of the players hit a three pointer.

"Your brothers made it my business."

"My brothers can't run my life. Much as they'd like to."

"I think you're afraid," he accused, and she felt the tightening of the muscles of her neck, the urge to defend herself.

"Of what?" she asked, but he didn't answer as the waitress appeared and slid their baskets onto the plank table, then offered up bottles of vinegar and ketchup. Only when they were alone again did Randi repeat herself. "You think I'm afraid of what?"

"Why don't *you* tell me. It's just odd, you know, for a woman not to tell the father of her child that he's a daddy. Goes against the grain. Usually the mother wants financial support. Emotional support. That kind of thing."

"I'm not usual," she said, and thought he whispered "Amen" under his breath, though she couldn't be certain as he covered up his comment with a long swallow of ale. She noticed the movement of his throat — dark with a bit of beard shadow as he swallowed — and something deep inside her, something dusky and wholly feminine, reacted. She drew her eyes away and told herself she was being a fool. It had been a long time since she'd been with a man, over a year now, but that didn't give her the right to ogle men like Kurt Striker nor imagine what it would feel like for him to touch her again, to kiss her, to press hot, insistent lips against the curve of her neck and push her sweater off her shoulder . . .

She caught herself and realized that he was watching her face, looking for her reaction. As if he could read her mind. To her horror she felt herself blush.

"Penny for your thoughts."

She shook her head, pretended interest in her meal by shaking vinegar over her fries. "Wouldn't sell 'em for a penny, or a nickel, or a thousand dollars."

"So tell me about the book," he suggested.

"The book?"

"The one you're writing. Another one of your secrets."

How could one man be so irritating? She ate in silence for a second and glowered across the table at him. "It's not a secret. I just didn't want to tell anyone about it until it was finished."

"You were on your way to the Flying M to finish it when you were forced off the road at Glacier National Park, right?" He dredged a piece of fish in tartar sauce.

She nodded.

"Think that's just a coincidence?"

"No one knew I was going to Montana to

write a book. Even the people at work thought I was just taking my maternity leave — which I was. I was planning to combine the two."

"Juanita at the ranch knew about it." He'd polished off one crispy lump of halibut and was working on a second.

"Of course she did. I already explained, it really wasn't a secret."

"If you say so." He ate in silence for a minute, but she didn't feel any respite, knew he was forming his next question, and sure enough, it came, hard and fast. "Tell me, Randi," he said, "who do you think wants to kill you?"

"I've been through this dozens of times with the police."

"Humor me." He was nearly finished with his food and she'd barely started. But her appetite had crumpled into nothing. She picked at her coleslaw. "Who are your worst enemies? You know, anyone who has a cause — just or not — for wanting you dead."

She'd considered the question over and over. It had run through her mind in an endless loop from the moment her memory had started working again when she'd awoken from her coma. "I . . . I don't know. No one has any reason to hate me enough to kill me."

"Murderers aren't always reasonable people," he pointed out.

"I can't name anyone."

"How about the baby's father? Maybe he found out you were pregnant, is ticked that you didn't tell him and, not wanting to be named as the father, decided to get rid of you both."

"He wouldn't do that."

"No?"

She shook her head. She wasn't certain about many things, but she doubted Joshua's father would care that he'd fathered a child, certainly wouldn't go through the steps to get rid of either of them. She felt a weight on her heart but ignored it as Striker, leaning back in the booth, pushed his near-empty basket aside. "If I'm going to help you, then I need to know everything that's going on. So who is he, Randi? Who's Joshua's daddy?"

She didn't realize she'd been shredding her napkin in her lap, but looked down and noticed all the pieces of red paper. She supposed she couldn't take her secret with her to the grave, but letting the world know the truth made her feel more vulnerable, that she was somehow breaching a special trust she had with her son.

"My money's on Donahue," he said

abruptly.

She froze.

He winked though his expression was hard. "I figure you'd go for the sexy-cowboy type."

"You don't know what my type is."

"Don't I?"

"Unfair, Striker, last night was . . . was . . ."

"What about it?"

"It was a mistake. We both know it. So, let's just forget it. As I said, you don't have any idea what 'my type' is."

One side of his mouth lifted in an irritating, sexy-as-hell smile. Green eyes held hers fast, and a wave, warm as a desert in August, climbed up her neck. "I'm workin' on it."

Her heart clenched. *Don't do this, Randi. Don't let him get to you. He's no better than . . . than . . .* Her throat tightened when she considered what a fool she'd been. For a man who'd seduced her. Used her. Cared less for her than he did for his dog. Silly, silly woman.

"Okay, Striker," she said, forcing the words through her lips, words she'd vowed only hours ago never to utter. "I'll tell you the truth," she said, hating the sense of relief it brought to be able to confide in someone. "But this is between you and me. Got it?

I'll tell you and you alone. When the time comes I'll tell Joshua's father and my brothers. But only when I say."

"Fair enough," he drawled, leaning back in his chair and folding his arms over his chest, all interest in his remaining French fries forgotten.

Randi took in a deep breath and prayed she wasn't making one of the biggest mistakes of her life. She stared Striker straight in the eye and admitted to him something she rarely acknowledged herself. "You're right. Okay? Joshua's father, and I use the term so loosely it's no longer coiled, is Sam Donahue." Her tongue nearly tripped over Sam's name. She didn't like saying it out loud, didn't like admitting that she, like too many others before her, had been swept off her feet by the charming, roguish cowboy. It was embarrassing and, had it not been for her precious son, a mistake she would have rued until her dying day. Joshua, of course, changed all that.

Striker didn't say a word. Nor had his lips curled in silent denunciation. And he didn't so much as lift an eyebrow in mockery. No. He played it straight, just observing her, watching her every reaction.

"So now you know," she said, standing. "I hope it helps, but I don't think it means anything. Thanks for dinner." She walked out of the bar and up the steps to the wet streets. The rain had turned to drizzle again, misting around the street lamps, and the air was heavy, laced with the brine from Puget Sound. Randi felt like running. As fast and far as she could. To get away from the claustrophobic feeling, the fear that compressed her chest, the very fear she'd tried to flee when she'd left Montana.

But it was with her wherever she went, she thought, her boots slapping along the rain-slick sidewalk as she hurried to her car. The city was far from deserted, traffic rushed through the narrow old streets and pedestrians bustled along the sidewalks. She carried no umbrella, didn't bother with her hood, let the dampness collect on her cheeks and flatten her hair. Not that she cared. Damn it, why had she told Striker about Sam Donahue? Her relationship with Sam hadn't really been a love affair, more of a fling, though at one time she'd been foolish enough to think she might be falling in love with the bastard. The favor hadn't been returned and she'd realized her mistake. But not before the pregnancy test had turned out positive.

She hadn't bothered to tell Donahue because she knew he wouldn't care. He was a selfish man by nature, a rambler who followed the rodeo circuit and didn't have time for the two ex-wives and children he'd already sired. Randi wasn't about to try to saddle him with the responsibility of another baby. She figured Joshua was better off with one strong parent than two who fought, living with the ghost of a father whom he would grow up not really knowing.

She knew her son would ask questions and she intended to answer them all honestly. When the time came. But not now . . . not when her baby was pure innocence.

"Randi!" Striker was at her side, his bare head as wet as her own, his expression hard.

"What? More questions?" she asked, unable to hide the sarcasm in her voice. "Well, sorry, but I'm fresh out of shocking little details about my life."

"I didn't come all the way to Seattle to embarrass you," he said as they rounded a final corner to the parking lot.

"That's how it seems."

"No, it doesn't. You know better."

She'd reached her Jeep and with a punch of the button on her remote, unlocked it once more. "Why do I have the feeling that you're not finished? That you won't be satisfied until you've stripped away every little piece of privacy I have."

"I just want to help."

He seemed sincere, but she'd been fooled before. By the master, Sam Donahue. Kurt Striker, damn him, was of the same ilk. Another cowboy. Another rogue. Another sexy man with a shadowy past. Another man she'd started to fall for. The kind to avoid. "Help?"

"That's right." His eyes shifted to her lips and she nervously licked them, tasting rainwater as it drizzled down her face. Her heart thudded. She knew in that second that he was going to kiss her. He was fighting it; she saw the battle in his eyes, but in the end raw emotion won out and his lips crashed down on hers so intensely she drew in a swift breath and it was followed quickly by his tongue. Slick. Sleek. Searching. The tip touched her teeth, forcing them apart as he grabbed her. Leather creaked, the sky parted, rain poured and Randi's foolish, foolish heart opened.

She kissed the rogue back, slamming her mind against thoughts that she was making the worst mistake of her life, that she was crossing a bridge that was burning behind her, that her life, from that moment on, would be changed forever.

But there, in the middle of the bustling

city, with raindrops falling on them both, she didn't care.

CHAPTER SEVEN

Stop this! Stop it now! Don't you remember last night?

Blinking against the rain, fighting the urge to lean against him, Randi pulled away from Kurt. "This is definitely not a good idea," she said. "It wasn't last night and it isn't now."

His mouth twisted. "I'm not sure about that."

"I am." It was a lie. Right now she wasn't certain of anything. She reached behind her and fumbled with the door handle. "Let's just give it a rest, okay?"

He didn't argue, nor did he stop her as she slid into the Jeep and, with shaking fingers, found her keys and managed to start the ignition. Lunacy. That's what it was. Sheer, unadulterated, pain-in-the-backside lunacy! She couldn't start kissing the likes of Kurt Striker again.

Dear God, what had she been thinking?

You weren't thinking. That's the problem!

She flipped on the radio, heard the first notes of a sappy love song and immediately punched the button to find talk radio, only to hear a popular program where a radio psychologist was giving out advice to someone who was mixed up with the wrong kind of man, the same kind of advice she handed out through her column in the *Clarion,* the very advice she should listen to herself.

First she'd made the mistake of getting involved with Sam Donahue and now she was falling for Kurt Striker . . . No! She pounded a fist on the steering wheel as she braked for a turnoff.

Cutting through traffic, she made a call on her cell phone to Sharon, was assured that Joshua was safe, then stopped at a local market for a few groceries.

Fifteen minutes later she pulled into the parking lot of her condo. Now away from the hustle and bustle of the city, the dark of the night seemed more threatening. The parking lot was dark and the security lamps were glowing, throwing pools of light onto the wet ground and a few parked cars. The parking area was deserted, none of her neighbors were walking dogs or taking out trash. Warm light glowed from only a few windows, the rest of the units were dark.

So what? This is why you chose this place. It was quiet, only a few units overlooking the lake.

For the first time since moving here, Randi looked at her darkened apartment and felt a moment's hesitation, a hint of fear. She glanced over her shoulder, through the back windows of the Jeep, wondering if someone was watching her, someone lurking in a bank of fir trees and rhododendron that ringed the parking lot, giving it privacy. She had the uneasy sensation that hidden eyes were watching her through a veil of wet needles and leaves.

"Get a grip," she muttered, hoisting the bag and holding tight to her key ring. As if it was some kind of protection. What a laugh!

No one was hiding. No one was watching her. And yet she wished she hadn't been so quick to put some distance between herself and Striker. Maybe she did need a bodyguard, someone she could trust.

Someone you can't keep your hands off of?

Someone you've made love to?

Someone that even now, even though you know better, you'd love to take to bed? In her mind's eye she saw the image of Kurt Striker, all taut skin and muscle as he held her in front of the dying fire.

Oh, for the love of St. Peter! Hauling her laptop, the groceries, her briefcase and her rebellious libido with her, she made her way to the porch, managed to unlock the door and snap on the interior lights. She almost wished Kurt was inside waiting for her again. But that was crazy. Nuts! She couldn't trust herself around that man.

"You're an idiot," she muttered, seeing her reflection in the mirror mounted by the coatrack in the front hall. Her hair was damp and curly with the rain, her cheeks flushed, her eyes bright. "This is just what got you into trouble in the first place." She dropped her computer and bag near her desk, shook herself out of her coat and heard a pickup roaring into the lot. Her silly heart leaped, but a quick glance through the kitchen window confirmed that Striker had returned. He was already out of the truck and headed toward the condo.

She met him at the front door.

"You don't seem to take a hint, do you?" she teased.

"Careful, woman, I'm not in the mood to have my chain yanked," he warned. "Traffic was a bitch."

He was inside in a second and bolted the door behind him. "I don't like it when you try to lose me."

"And I don't like being manhandled." She started unpacking groceries, stuffing a carton of milk into the near-empty refrigerator.

"I kissed you."

"On the street, when I obviously didn't want you to."

One of his eyebrows lifted in disbelief. "You didn't want it?" He snorted. "I'd love to see what you were like when you did."

"That was last night," she reminded him, then mentally kicked herself. Lifting a hand, she stopped any argument he might have. "Let's not talk about last night."

He kicked out a bar stool and plopped himself at the counter that separated the kitchen from the living room. "Okay, but there is something we need to discuss."

She braced herself. "Which is?"

"Sam Donahue."

"Another off-limits subject." She pulled a loaf of bread from the wet sack.

"I don't think so. We've wasted enough time as it is and I'm getting sick of you not being straight with me."

"I should never have told you."

He shot her a condemning look. "I'd already guessed, remember?" He took a deep breath and ran stiff fingers through his hair. "You got any wood for that?" he asked, hitching his chin toward the fireplace.

"A little. In a closet on the back deck."

"Get me a beer, I'll make a fire and then, whether you like it or not, we're going to discuss your ex-lover."

"Gee," she mocked, "and who said single women don't have any fun? You know, Striker, you've got a helluva nerve to barge in here and start barking orders. Just because . . . because of what happened last night, you don't have the right to start bossing me around in my own home."

"You're right," he said without a trace of regret carved into his features. "Would you please get me a beer and I'll get the firewood."

"I might be out of beer. I didn't pick any up at the store."

"There's one left. In the door of the fridge. I checked earlier." The empty bottle on the coffee table stood as testament to that very fact.

"When you practiced breaking and entering," she muttered as he kicked back the stool and made his way to the deck. She opened the refrigerator again and saw the single long-neck in the door. The guy was observant. But still a bully who had barged unwelcome into her life. A sexy bully at that. Her worst nightmare.

She yanked out the last beer, twisted off the top and, as he carried in a couple of chunks of oak to the fire, took a long swallow. The least he could do was share, she decided, watching as he bent on the tiled hearth, his jacket and shirt riding up over his belt and jeans, offering her the view of a slice of his taut, muscular back. Her throat was suddenly dry as dust and she took another pull from the long-neck. What the hell was she going to do with him? She'd already bared her soul and her body, then, after insisting that she wasn't interested in him, kissed him on the street as if she never wanted to stop, and now . . . She slid a glance toward the cracked door of her bedroom and in her mind she saw them together, wrapped in the sheets, sweaty bodies tangled and heaving as he kissed her breasts. Her heart pounded as he pulled at her nipple, his hands sliding down to sculpt her waist as he mounted her, gently nudging her knees apart, readying himself above her, his erection stiff, his green gaze fiery. Then, eyes locked, he entered her in one long, hard thrust —

He cleared his throat and she was brought back to the living area of her condo where he was still tending to the fire. Turning, she blushed as she realized he'd said something to her. For the life of her she couldn't remember a word. "Wh-what?"

"I asked if you had a match." His gaze was on her face, then traveled down the short corridor to the bedroom. Amusement caused an eyebrow to arch and she wanted to die. No doubt he could read her embarrassing thoughts.

"Oh, yeah . . ." While she'd been fantasizing, he'd crumpled old newspaper and stacked the firewood, even splintering off some pieces of kindling.

She took another swallow, handed him the bottle and hurried into the kitchen where she rummaged through a drawer. *Don't go there. You're not going to tumble into bed with him. Not again. You're not even going to kiss him again. You're not going to do anything stupid with him. No more.* She found a pack of matches and tossed them over the counter to him, all the while trying to quell the hammering of her heart. Time to go on the offensive.

"Okay, Striker, so now I've told you my darkest secret. What's yours?"

"None of your business."

"Wait a minute. That's not fair."

"You're right, it's not." He struck a match and the smell of sulfur singed the air as he touched the tiny flame to the dry paper and

111

the fire crackled to life. "But then not much is."

"You said I could ask you anything when we were in the pub."

"I changed my mind."

"Just like that?" she asked incredulously as she snapped her fingers.

"Uh-huh." He took a long pull from the bottle.

"No way. I think I deserve to know who the hell you are."

Rocking back on his heels as the fire caught, he looked up at her standing on the other side of the counter. "I'm an ex-cop turned P.I."

"I already figured that much. But what about your personal life?"

"It's private."

"You're single, right? There's no Mrs. Striker."

He hesitated enough to cause her heart to miss a beat. *Oh, God, not again,* she thought as she leaned against the counter for support. He'd kissed her. Touched her. Made love to her.

"Not anymore. I was married but it ended a few years back."

"Why?"

His jaw tightened. "Haven't you read the statistics?"

"I'm talking about the reason behind the statistics, at least in your case."

A shadow passed behind his eyes and he said, "It just didn't work out. I was a cop. Probably paid more attention to the job than my wife."

"And you didn't have any kids?"

Again the hesitation. Again the shadow. His lips tightened at the corners as he stood and dusted his hands. "I don't have any children," he said slowly, "and I never hear from my ex. That about covers it all, doesn't it?" There was just a spark of challenge in his eyes, daring her to argue with him. A dozen questions bubbled up in her throat, but she held them back. For now. There were other ways to get information about him. She was a reporter, for God's sake. She had the means to find out just about anything that had happened to him. Newsworthy articles would be posted on the Internet, personal stuff through other sources.

With Sam Donahue she'd been trusting and it had backfired in her face, but this time . . . Oh, God, why was she even thinking like this? There was no *this time!* There was no Kurt Striker in her life except as an irritating bodyguard her brothers had hired. That was it. He was here because he was hired to be here; she was a job to him. Nothing more.

"Look, I've got to get some work done," she said, motioning to her laptop. "I've been gone for months and if I don't answer some e-mail and put together a new column or two, I'm going to be in big trouble. My boss and I are already not real tight. So, if you don't mind . . . well, even if you do, I'm going to start plowing through what's been piling up. I understand that you think you've got to be with me 24/7, but it's not necessary. No one's going to take a potshot at me here."

"Why would you think that?" Striker drained the rest of his beer.

"Because there are too many people around, there's a security guard for the condos always on the premises, and most importantly, Joshua is safe with Sharon."

The expression on his face told her he was of another mind. And wasn't she, really? Hadn't she, just minutes ago in the parking lot, sensed that someone had been watching her? She rounded the counter as he straightened and crossed the room.

"Look, I do know that I'm in some kind of danger," she said. "Obviously I know it or I wouldn't have taken the time to hide the baby. I came back here to try to figure this out, to take the heat off my brothers, to get on with my life and let them get on with theirs. And yeah, I'd be lying if I didn't say I was nervous, that I wasn't starting to jump at shadows, but I need to sort through some things, get a handle on what's happening."

"That's why I'm here. I'm thinking that maybe if we work together, we can make some sense of what's going on." He was close to her, near enough that she could smell the wet leather of his jacket, see the striations of color in his green eyes, feel the heat of his body.

She couldn't even make sense of the moment. "That might be impossible. I've been thinking about what happened from every angle and I come up with the same conclusion. I don't have any real enemies that I know of. At least not anyone who would want to hurt me and my family. It doesn't make any sense." To put some distance between her body and his, she walked to the couch and flung herself onto the cushions. *Who? What? Why?* The questions that had haunted her nights and caused her to lose sleep were still unanswered as they rolled around in her brain.

"So what does make sense?" he demanded. "Someone followed you from Seattle and on your way to Grand Hope, Montana, forced you off the road. Why?"

"I told you, I don't know. Believe me, I've been thinking about it."

"Think harder." He frowned and rammed stiff fingers through hair that was still damp. "If it doesn't have to do with the baby, then what about your job? Did you give someone bad advice and really tick someone off?"

She shook her head. "I thought about that, too. When I was back in Montana, I got on-line and searched through the columns for the two months prior to the accident and I couldn't find anything that would infuriate a person."

His head snapped up. "So you are worried?"

"Of course I'm worried. Who wouldn't be? But there was nothing in any of the advice I gave that would cause someone to snap."

"You think. There are always nutcases." He set his empty bottle on the counter.

That much was true, she thought wearily. "But none who have e-mailed me, or called me, or contacted me in any way. I double-checked every communication I received." He nodded and she realized that he'd probably been privy to that information as well.

"Well, there's got to be a reason. We're just missing it." He was thinking hard; she could tell by the way he rubbed his chin.

"You write magazine articles under a pseudonym."

"Nothing controversial."

His eyes narrowed. "What about the book you were working on?"

She hesitated. The manuscript she was writing wasn't finished and she'd taken great pains to keep it secret while she investigated a payola scam on the rodeo circuit. It was while researching the book that she'd met Sam Donahue, a friend, he'd claimed, of her brothers'. As it turned out he hadn't been as much a friend as an acquaintance and somehow she'd ended up falling for him, knowing him to be a rogue, realizing that part of his charm was the hint of danger around him, and yet she'd tumbled into bed with him anyway. And ended up pregnant.

Which had been a blessing in disguise, of course. Without her ill-fated affair with Sam, she never would have had Joshua, and that little guy was the light of her life.

"What's in the book that's so all-fired important?"

Sighing, she walked to the couch and dropped into the soft cushions. "You know what's in it for the most part."

"A book on cowboys."

"Well, a little more than that." Leaning

her head back, she closed her eyes. "It's about all aspects of rodeos, the good, the bad, the ugly. Especially the ugly. Along with all the rah-rah for a great American West tradition, there's also the dark side to it all, the seamy underbelly. As I was getting information, I learned about the drugs, animal abuse, cheating, payola, you name it."

"And let me guess, most of the information came from good old Sam Donahue."

"Some of it," she admitted, opening an eye and catching Kurt scowling, as if the mere mention of Donahue's name made Striker see red. "I was going to name names in my book and, I suppose, I could have made a few people nervous. But the thing of it was, no one really knew what I was doing."

"Donahue?"

She shook her head and glanced to the window. "I told him it was a series of articles about small-town celebrations, that rodeos were only a little bit of the slice of Americana I was going to write about. Sam wasn't all that interested in what I was doing."

"Why not?"

"Oh, I don't know," she said, turning her attention to Kurt. The fire was burning softly, casting golden shadows on the cozy rooms. She snapped on a table lamp, hoping to break the feeling of intimacy the flames created. "Maybe it's because Sam's an egomaniac and pretty much consumed with his own life."

"Sounds charming," he mocked.

"I thought so. At first. But it did wear thin fast."

Striker lifted an eyebrow and she added, "I'd already realized that it wasn't going to work out when I suspected I was pregnant."

"What did he say about it?"

"Nothing. He never knew."

"You didn't tell him."

"That's right. Didn't we go over this before?"

Striker looked as if he wanted to say something but held his tongue. For that she was grateful. She didn't need any judgment calls.

"Besides," she added with more than a trace of bitterness, "I figure we're even now. He forgot to mention that he wasn't really divorced from his last wife when he started dating me." She wrinkled her nose and felt that same old embarrassment that had been with her from the moment she'd realized Sam had lied, that he'd been married all the time he'd chased after her, swearing that he was divorced.

Fool that she'd been, she'd fallen for him and believed every word that had tripped over his lying tongue.

Now a blush stole up her neck and she bit down on her back teeth. She'd always been proud of her innate intelligence, but when it came to men, she'd often been an idiot. She'd chosen poorly, trusted too easily, fallen harder than she should have. From Teddy Sherman, the ranch hand her father had hired when she was seventeen, to a poet and a musician in college, and finally Sam Donahue, the rough-and-tumble cowpoke who'd turned out to be a lying bastard if ever there was one. Well, no more, she told herself even as Kurt Striker, damn him, threatened to break down her defenses.

He walked to the fire, grabbed a poker and jabbed at the burning logs. Sparks drifted upward through the flue and one of the blackened chunks of oak split with a soft thud.

Randi watched him and felt that same sense of yearning, a tingle of desire, she'd experienced every time she was around him. She sensed something different in Kurt, a strength of character that had been lacking in the other men she'd found enchanting. They had been dreamers, or, in the case of Donahue, cheats, but she didn't think either was a part of Striker's personality. His boots seemed securely planted on the ground rather than drifting into the clouds, and he appeared intensely honest. His eyes were clear, his shoulders straight, his smile, when he offered it, not as sly as it was amused. He appealed to her at a whole new level. Man to woman, face-to-face, not looking down at her, nor elevating her onto a pedestal from which she would inevitably fall.

"So what do you think about your kid?" he asked suddenly as he straightened and dusted his hands.

"I'm nuts about him, of course."

"Do you really think he's safe with the Okano woman?"

"I wouldn't have left him there if I didn't."

"I'd feel better if he was with you. With me."

"No one followed me to Sharon's. Not many people know we're friends. She was in my dorm in college and just moved up here last fall. I . . . I really think he's safer there. I've already driven her nuts calling her. She thinks I'm paranoid and I'm not so sure she's wrong."

"Paranoid isn't all that bad. Not in this case." Striker reached into his jacket pocket, flipped open his cell and dialed. A few seconds later he was engrossed in a conversation, ordering someone to watch Sharon Okano's apartment as well as do some digging on Sam Donahue. ". . . that's right. I want to know for certain where he was on the dates that Randi was run off the road and someone attempted to kill her in the hospital . . . Yeah, I know he had an alibi, but double-check and don't forget to dig into some of the thugs he hangs out with. This could have been a paid job . . . I don't know but start with Marv Bates and Charlie . . . Damn, what's his name, Charlie —"

"Caldwell," Randi supplied, inwardly shuddering at the thought of the two cowboys Sam had introduced her to. Marv was whip thin with lips that barely moved when he talked and eyes that were forever narrowed. Charlie was a lug, a big, fleshy man who could surprise you with how fast he could move if properly motivated.

"That's right, Charlie Caldwell. Check prison records. See if any of Donahue's buddies have done time. . . . Okay . . . You can reach me on the cell, that would be best." He was walking to the desk. "I'll be in the condo, but let's not use the landline. I checked, it doesn't appear bugged, but I'm not sure."

Randi's blood chilled at the thought that

someone could have tampered with her phone lines or crept into her home while she was away. But then Striker hadn't had any problem getting inside. He might not have been the first. Her skin crawled as she looked over her belongings with new eyes. Suede couch, faux leopard-print chair and ottoman, antique rocker, end tables she'd found in a secondhand store and her great-grandmother's old treadle sewing machine that stood near the window. The cacti were thriving, the Boston fern shedding and near death, the mirror over her fireplace, the one she'd inherited from her mother, still chipped in one corner. Nothing out of place. Nothing to give her pause.

And yet . . . something wasn't right. Something she couldn't put her finger on. Just like the eerie sensation that she was being watched when she parked her Jeep.

"Later." Striker snapped the phone shut and watched as Randi walked to her desk, double-checking that nothing had been disturbed. She'd already done a quick once-over when she'd come home earlier, but now, knowing that her phone could have been tapped, her home violated, her life invaded by an unknown assailant, she wanted to make certain that everything was as it should be.

Her phone rang and she nearly jumped through the roof. She snagged the receiver before it could jangle a second time.

"Hello?" she said, half expecting a deep-throated voice on the other end to issue a warning, or heavy breathing to be her only response.

"So you did get home!"

Randi nearly melted at the sound of Slade's voice. He was her youngest half brother, closest to her in age. Slade had been born with the same McCafferty wild streak that had cursed all of John Randall's children. Slade had just held on to his untamed ways longer than his older brothers.

"I thought you'd have the brains to call and tell us you'd arrived safely," he admonished, and she felt a twinge of guilt.

"I guess I hadn't gotten around to it," she said, smiling at the thought of her brothers, who had once resented her, now fretting over her.

"Is everything all right?"

"So far, although I have a bone to pick with you."

"Uh-oh."

"And Matt and Thorne."

"It figures."

"Who the hell do you think you are hiring

124

a bodyguard for me behind my back?" she demanded and saw, in the mirror's reflection, Kurt Striker standing behind her. Their eyes met and there was something in his gaze that seemed to bore straight into hers, to touch her soul.

Slade was trying to explain. "You need someone to help you —"

"You mean I need a *man* to watch over me," she cut in, irritated all over again. Frustrated, she turned her attention to the window, where just beyond the glass she could make out the angry waters of Lake Washington roiling in the darkness. "Well, for your information, brother dear, I can take care of myself."

"Yeah, right."

Slade's sarcasm cut deep.

Involuntarily, she squared her shoulders. "I'm serious."

"So are we."

Randi heard conversation in the background, not only the deep rumble of male voices, but others as well, the higher pitches of her sisters-in-law, no doubt, and rising above the rest of the conversation, the sharp staccato burst of Spanish that could only have come from Juanita, the housekeeper.

"You tell her to be careful. *Dios!* What was she thinking running off like that!"

125

More Spanish erupted and Slade said, "Did you hear that? Juanita thinks —"

"I heard what she said." Randi felt a pang of homesickness, which was just plain ludicrous. This was her home. Where she belonged. She had a life here in Seattle. At the newspaper. Here in this condo. And yet, as she stared out the window to the white-caps whirling furiously on the black water, she wondered if she had made a mistake in returning to this bustling city that she'd fallen in love with years before. She liked the crowds. The noise. The arts. The history. The beauty of Puget Sound and the briny smell of the sea when she walked or jogged near the waterfront.

But her brothers weren't here.

Nor were Nicole, Kelly or Jamie, her new sisters-in-law. They'd become friends and she missed them as well as Nicole's daughters and the ranch and . . .

Suddenly stiffening her spine, she pushed back all her maudlin thoughts. She was doing the right thing. Reclaiming her life. Trying to figure out who was hell-bent on harming her and her family. "Tell everyone I'm fine. Okay? A big girl. And I don't appreciate you and Thorne and Matt hiring Striker."

"Well, that's just too damn bad now, isn't

it?" he said, reigniting her anger.

Her headache was throbbing again, she was so tired she wanted to sink into her bed and never wake up and, more than anything, she wished she could reach through the phone lines and shake some sense into her brothers. "You know, Slade, you really can be a miserable son of a bitch."

"I try," he drawled in that damnable country-boy accent that was usually accompanied by a devilish twinkle in his eyes.

She imagined his lazy smile. "Nice, Slade. Do you want to talk to your new employee?" Without waiting for an answer, she slammed the phone into Kurt Striker's hand and stormed to her bedroom. This was insane, but she was tired of arguing about it, was bound and determined to get on with her life. She had a baby to take care of and a job to do.

But what if they're all right? What if someone really is after you? After Joshua? Didn't you think someone had already broken into this place?

Her gaze swept the bedroom. Nothing seemed disturbed . . . or did it? Had she left the curtains to the back deck parted? Had her closet door been slightly ajar . . . ? She lifted her eyes, caught a glimpse of her reflection and saw a shadow of fear pass behind her own eyes. God, she hated this.

She heard footsteps approaching and then, in the glass, saw Kurt walking down the short hallway and stop at the bedroom door.

Her throat was suddenly dry as cotton and inadvertently she licked her lips. His gaze flickered to the movement and the corners of his mouth tightened, and just the hint of desperation, of lust, darkened his eyes.

For a split second their gazes locked. Held. Randi's pulse jumped, as if it were suddenly a living, breathing thing. Her heartbeat thundered in her ears. Inside, she felt a twinge, the hint of a dangerous craving she'd experienced last night.

She knew that it would only take a glance, a movement, a whisper and he would come inside, close the door, take her into his arms and kiss her as if she'd never been kissed before. It would be hard, raw, desperate and they would oh so easily tumble onto the bed and make love for hours.

His lips compressed.

He took a step inside.

She could barely breathe.

He reached forward, grabbed hold of the doorknob.

Her knees went weak.

Oh, God, she wanted him. Imagined

touching him, lying with him, feeling the heat of his body. "Kurt, I . . ."

"Shh, darlin'," he said, his voice as rough as sandpaper. "It's been a long day. Why don't you get some rest." He offered her a wink that caused her heart to crack. "I'll be in the living room if you need me." He pulled the door shut tight and she listened to the sound of his footsteps retreating down the short hallway.

Slowly she let out the breath she'd been holding and sagged onto the bed. Disappointment mingled with relief. It would be a mistake of epic proportions to make love to him. She knew it. They both did. On unsteady legs she walked into the bathroom and opened the medicine cabinet. She reached for a bottle of ibuprofen and stopped short.

What if someone had been in her home?

What if someone had tampered with her over-the-counter medications? Her food?

"Now you really are getting paranoid," she muttered, as she poured the pills into the toilet and flushed them down.

Paranoid, maybe.

But alive for certain.

Making her way back to the bedroom, she slid under the covers and decided that she could work with Striker or against him.

With him would be a lot more interesting. And together they might be able to get through the nightmare that had become her life.

CHAPTER EIGHT

He was lying next to her, his body hard and honed, skin stretched taut over muscles that were smooth and fluid as he levered up on one elbow to stare down at her. Green eyes glittered with a dark seductive fire that thrilled her and silently spoke of pleasures to come. With the fingers of one callused hand he traced the contours of her body. She tingled, her breasts tightening under his scrutinizing gaze, her nipples becoming hard as buttons. He leaned forward and scraped a beard-roughened cheek over her flesh. Deep inside, she felt desire stretching as it came awake.

This was so wrong. She shouldn't be in bed with Kurt Striker. What had she been thinking? How had this happened? She barely knew the man . . . and yet, the wanting was so intense, burning through her blood, chasing away her doubts, and as he bent to kiss her, she knew she couldn't resist, that with just the brush of his hard lips on hers she would be lost completely —

Bam!

Her eyes flew open at the sound. Where was she? It was dark. And cold. She was alone in the bed — her bed — and she felt as if she'd slept for hours, her bladder stretched to the limit, her stomach rumbling for food.

"Let's go, Sleeping Beauty," Kurt said from the vicinity of the doorway. She blinked and found him standing in the doorway, his shoulders nearly touching each side of the frame, his body backlit by the flickering light still cast from the living-room fire. In relief he seemed larger, more rugged. The kind of man to avoid.

So she'd been dreaming about making love to him again. Only dreaming. Thank God. Not that the ache deep within her had subsided. Yes, she was in her own bed, but she was alone and fully dressed, just the way he'd left her minutes — or had it been hours — before?

"Wha — What's the rush?" she mumbled, trying to shake off the remainder of that damnably erotic fantasy even though a part of her wanted to close her eyes and call it back. "So what happened to 'shh, darlin', you should get some rest'?" she asked sarcastically.

He took a step into the room. "You got it. Slept for nearly eighteen hours, now it's time to rock 'n' roll."

"What? Eighteen hours . . . no . . ." She glanced at the bedside clock and the digital display indicated it was after three. "I couldn't have . . ." But the bad taste in her mouth and the pressure on her bladder suggested he was right.

Groaning, she thought about her job and the fact that she was irreparably late. Bill Withers was probably chewing her up one side and down the other. "I'm gonna get fired yet," she muttered, then added, "Give me a sec."

Scrambling from beneath the warmth of her duvet, she stumbled over one of her shoes on her way to the bathroom. Once inside, she shut the door, snapped on the light and cringed at her reflection. Within minutes she'd relieved herself, splashed water onto her face and brushed her teeth. Her face was a disaster, her short hair sticking up at all angles. The best she could do was wet it down and scrub away the smudges of mascara that darkened her eyes.

Thankfully her headache was gone and she was thinking more clearly as she opened the door to the bedroom and found Kurt leaning against the frame, a strange look on his face. She yawned. "What?" she asked and then she knew. With drop-dead certainty. Her heart nearly stopped. "It's the baby," she said, fear suddenly gelling her blood. "Joshua. What's wrong? Is he okay?"

"He's fine."

"How do you know?"

"I'm having Sharon Okano's place watched."

She was stunned and suddenly frantic and reached for the shoe she'd nearly tripped over. "You really think something might happen to him?"

"Let's just say I don't want to take any chances."

She crammed the shoe onto her foot, then bent down, peering under the bed for its mate. Her mind was clearing a bit as she found the missing shoe and slid it on. Striker was jumping at shadows, that was it. Joshua was fine. Fine. He had to be.

"Donahue's in town."

She rocked back on her heels. The news hit her like a ton of bricks, but she tried to stay calm. "How do you know?"

"He was spotted."

"By whom?"

"Someone working for me."

"Working for you. Did my brothers hire an entire platoon of security guards or something?"

"Eric Brown and I have known each other for years. He's been watching Sharon Okano's place."

"What? Wait! You've got someone spying on her?"

His face was rigid. "I'm not ready to take any chances."

"Don't you think someone lurking around will just draw attention to the place? You know, like waving some kind of red flag."

"He's a little more discreet than that."

She shook her head, clearing out the cobwebs, trying to keep her rising sense of panic at bay. "Wait a minute. This doesn't make any sense. Sam doesn't know about Joshua. He has no idea that I was pregnant . . . and probably wouldn't have cared one way or the other had he found out."

"You think."

"I'm pretty damn sure." She straightened.

"Then why would he be cruising by Sharon Okano's place?"

"Oh, God, I don't know." Her remaining calm quickly evaporated. She had to get to her baby, to see that he was all right. She made a beeline for the closet. "This is making less and less sense," she muttered and was already reaching for a jacket. Glancing at her shoes, she saw a pair of black cowboy

135

boots, one of which had fallen over. Boots she hadn't worn since high school. Boots her father had given her and she'd never had the heart to give away. Ice slid through her veins as she walked closer and saw that the dust that had accumulated over the toes had been disturbed. Her throat went dry. "Dear God."

Kurt had followed her into the walk-in. He was pulling an overnight bag from an upper shelf. "Randi?" he asked, his voice filled with concern. "What?"

"Someone was in here." Fear mixed with fury. "I mean . . . unless when you got here you came into my closet and decided to try on my cowboy boots."

"Your boots?" His gaze swept the interior of the closet to land upon the dusty black leather.

"I haven't touched them in months and look —"

He was already bending down and seeing for himself. "You're sure that you didn't —"

"No. I'm telling you someone was in here!" She tamped down the panic that threatened her, and fought the urge to kick at something. No one had the right to break into her home. No one.

"Who else has a key?"

"To this place?"

"Yes."

"Just me."

"Not Donahue?"

"No!"

"Sharon? Your brothers?"

She was shaking her head violently. Was the man dense? "I'm telling you I never gave anyone a key, not even to come in and water the plants."

"What about a neighbor, just in case you lost yours?"

"No! Geez, Striker, don't you get it? It's just me. I even changed the locks when I bought the place so the previous owner doesn't have a set rattling around in some drawer somewhere."

"Where do you keep the spare?"

"One with me. One in the car. Another in my top desk drawer."

He was already headed down the hallway and into the living room with Randi right on his heels.

"Show me."

"Here." Reaching around him, she pulled open the center drawer, felt until her fingers scraped against cold metal, then pulled the key from behind a year-old calendar. "Right where I left it."

"And the one in your car."

"I don't know. It was with me when I had

137

the accident. I assume it was in the wreck-age."

"You didn't ask the police?"

"I was in a coma, remember? When I woke up I was a mess, broken bones, internal injuries, and I had amnesia."

"The police inventoried everything in the car when it was impounded, so they must've found the key, right?" he insisted.

"I . . . Geez, I'm not sure, but I don't think it was on the report. I saw it. I even have a copy somewhere."

"Back at the Flying M?"

"No — I cleared everything out when I left. It's here somewhere." She located her briefcase and riffled through the pockets until she found a manila envelope. Inside was a copy of the police report about the accident and the inventory receipt for the impounded car. She skimmed the documents quickly.

Road maps, registration, insurance information, three sixty-seven in change, a pair of sunglasses and a bottle of glass cleaner, other miscellaneous items but no key ring. "They didn't find it."

"And you didn't ask."

She whirled on him, crumpling the paper in her fist. "I already told you, I was laid up. I didn't think about it."

"Hell." Kurt's lips compressed into a blade-thin line. His eyes narrowed angrily. "Come on." He pocketed the key, slammed the drawer shut and stormed down the hallway to the bedroom. In three swift strides he was inside the closet again. He unzipped the overnight bag and handed it to her. "Here. Pack a few things. Quickly. And don't touch the damn boots." He disappeared again and she heard him banging in the kitchen before he returned with a plastic bag and started carefully sliding it over the dusty cowboy boots. "I've already got your laptop and your briefcase in the truck."

Suddenly she understood. He wanted her to leave. Now. His jaw was set, his expression hard as granite. "Now, wait a minute. I'm not leaving town. Not yet." Things were moving too quickly, spinning out of control. "I just got home and I can't up and take off again. I've got responsibilities, a life here."

"We'll only be gone for a night or two. Until things cool off."

"We? As in you and me?"

"And the baby."

"And go where?"

"Someplace safe."

"This is my home."

"And someone's been in here. Someone

with the key."

"I can change the locks, Striker. I've got a job and a home and —"

"And someone stalking you."

She opened her mouth to argue, then snapped it closed. She had to protect her baby. No matter what else. Yes, she needed to find out who was hell-bent on terrorizing her, but her first priority was to keep Joshua safe, and the truth of the matter was, Randi was already out of her mind with worry. Striker's concerns only served to fuel her anxiety. She was willing to bet he wasn't the kind of man to panic easily. And he was visibly upset. Great. She began throwing clothes into the overnight bag. "I can't take any chances with Joshua," she said.

"I know." His voice had a hint of kindness tucked into the deep timbre and she had to remind herself that he'd been hired to be concerned. Though she didn't believe that the money he'd been promised was his sole motivation in helping her, it certainly was a factor. If he kept both her and her son's skins intact, Striker's wallet would be considerably thicker. "Let's get a move on."

She was through arguing for the moment. No doubt Striker had been in more than his share of tight situations. If he really felt it was necessary to take her and her son and hide out for a while, so be it. She zipped the bag closed and ripped a suede jacket from its hanger. Was it her imagination or did it smell slightly of cigarette smoke?

Now she was getting paranoid. No one had been wearing her jacket. That was nuts.

Gritting her teeth, she fought the sensation that she'd been violated, that an intruder had pried into her private space. "I assume you've got some kind of plan."

"Yep." He straightened, the boots properly bagged.

"And that you're going to share it with me."

"Not yet."

"You can't tell me?"

"Not right now."

"Why not?"

"It's better if you don't know."

"Oh, right, keep the little woman in the dark. That's always a great idea," she said sarcastically. "This isn't the Dark Ages, Striker."

If possible, his lips compressed even further. His mouth was the thinnest of lines, his jaw set, his expression hard as nails. And then she got it. Why he was being so tight-lipped. "Wait a minute. What do you think? That this place is bugged?"

When he didn't answer, she shook her

head. Disbelieving. "No way."

He threw her a look that cut her to the bone. "Let's get a move on."

She didn't argue, just dug through the drawers of her dresser and threw some essentials into her bag, then grabbed her purse.

Within minutes they were inside Kurt's truck and roaring out of the parking lot. Yesterday's rain had stopped, but the sky was still overcast, gray clouds moving slowly inland from the Pacific. Randi stared out the window, but her mind was racing. Could Sam have found out about Joshua? It was possible, of course, that he'd somehow learned she'd had a baby, but she doubted he would do the math to figure out if he was the kid's father. The truth of the matter was that he just didn't give a damn. Never had. She drummed her fingers against window.

"I don't know why you think just because Donahue's in town that Joshua's not safe. If he drove by, it was probably just a fluke, a coincidence. Believe me, Sam Donahue wouldn't give two cents that he fathered another kid." She leaned against the passenger door as Kurt inched the pickup through the tangle of thick traffic.

"A truck belonging to Donahue has

cruised by Sharon Okano's apartment complex twice this afternoon. Not just once. I wouldn't call that a coincidence. Would you?"

"No." Her throat went dry, her fingers curled into balls of tension.

"Already checked the plates with the DMV. That's what tipped Brown off, the license plates were from out of state. Montana."

Randi's entire world cracked. She fingered the chain at her throat. "But he's rarely there, in Montana," she heard herself saying as if from a long distance away. "And I didn't tell him about Joshua."

"Doesn't matter what you told him. He could have found out easy enough. He has ties to Grand Hope. Parents, an ex-wife or two. Gossip travels fast. It doesn't take a rocket scientist to count back nine months from the date your baby was born." Striker managed to nose the truck onto the freeway where he accelerated for less than a mile, then slammed on the brakes as traffic stopped and far in the distance lights from a police car flashed bright.

"Great," Striker muttered, forcing the truck toward the next exit. He pulled his cell phone from the pocket of his jacket and poked in a number. A few seconds later, he said, "Look, we're caught in traffic. An accident northbound. It's gonna be awhile. Stay where you are and call me if the rig goes by or if there's any sign of Donahue."

Randi listened and tried not to panic. So Sam Donahue was in the area. It wasn't as if he never came to Seattle. Hadn't she hooked up with him here, in a bar on the waterfront? She'd been doing research on her book and had realized through the wonders of the Internet that he'd been in a rodeo competition in Oregon and was traveling north on his way to Alberta, Canada. She'd e-mailed him, met him for a drink and the rest was history.

"Good. Just keep an eye out. We'll be there ASAP." Striker snapped the phone shut and slid a glance in her direction. "Donahue hasn't been back."

"Maybe I should call him."

A muscle in Kurt's jaw leaped as he glared through the windshield. "And why the hell would you want to do that?"

"To find out what he's doing in town."

Striker's eyes narrowed. "You'd call up the guy who's trying to kill you."

"We don't know that he's trying to kill me." She shook her head and leaned the back of her crown against the seat rest. "It doesn't make sense. Even if he knew about

Joshua, Sam wouldn't want anything to do with him."

"So why did you two break up — wait a minute, let's start with how you got together."

"I'd always wanted to write a book and my brothers had not only glamorized the whole rodeo circuit but they had also told me about the seedy side. There were illegal wagers, lots of betting. Some contestants would throw a competition, others drugged their horses, or their competitors' mounts. The animals — bulls, calves, horses — were sometimes mistreated. It's a violent sport, one that attracts macho men and competitive women moving from one town to the next. There are groupies and bar fights and prescription and recreational drug abuse. A lot of these cowboys live in pain and there's the constant danger of being thrown and trampled or gored or crushed. High passion. I thought it would make for interesting reading, so, while interviewing people, I came across Sam Donahue." Her tongue nearly tripped on his name. "He grew up in Grand Hope, knew my brothers, was even on the circuit with Matt. I started interviewing him, one thing led to another and . . . well, the rest, as they say, is history."

"How'd you find him?"

"I read about a local rodeo, down towards Centralia. He was entered, so I got his number, gave him a call and agreed to meet him for a drink. My brothers didn't much like him but I found him interesting and charming. We had a connection in that we both grew up in Montana, and I was coming off a bad relationship, so we hit it off. In retrospect, I'd probably say it was a mistake, except for the fact that I ended up with Joshua. My son is worth every second of heartache I suffered."

"What kind of heartache?" Striker asked, his jaw rock hard.

She glanced through the window, avoiding his eyes. "Oh, you know. The kind where you find out that the last ex-wife wasn't quite an ex. Sam had never quite gotten around to signing the divorce papers." She felt a fool for having believed the lying son of a bitch. She'd known better. She was a journalist, for crying out loud. She should have checked him out, seen the warning signs, because she'd always made a point of dating men who were completely single — not engaged, not separated, not seriously connected with any woman. But she'd failed with Sam Donahue, believing him when he'd lied and said he'd been separated two years, divorced for six months.

146

Striker was easing the truck past the accident where the driver of a tow truck was winching a mangled Honda onto its bed and a couple of police officers were talking with two men near the twisted front end of a minivan of some kind. A paramedic truck was parked at an angle and two officers were talking with several boys in baseball hats who appeared unhurt but shaken. As soon as the truck was past the accident, traffic cleared and Striker pushed the speed limit again.

"So you didn't know he was married."

"Right," she replied, but couldn't stop the heat from washing up the back of her neck. She'd been a fool. "I knew that he was divorced from his first wife, Corrine. Patsy was his second wife. Might still be for all I know. Once I found out he was still married I was outta there." With one finger she drew on the condensation on the passenger-door window.

"You loved him." There it was. The statement she'd withdrawn from; the one she couldn't face.

Striker's fingers were coiled in a death grip around the steering wheel, as if somehow her answer mattered to him.

"I thought I loved him, but . . . even while we were seeing each other, I knew it wasn't right. There was something off." It was hard to explain that tumble of emotions. "The trouble was, by the time I'd figured it out, I was pregnant."

"So you decided to keep the baby and the secret."

"Yes," she admitted, strangely relieved to unburden herself as Striker took an off-ramp and cut through the neighborhood where Sharon Okano's apartment was located. She hesitated about telling him the rest of the story, but decided to trust him with the truth. "Along with the fact that Sam didn't tell me he was married, he also failed to mention that he and some of his friends had actually drugged a competitor's animals just before the competition. One bull reacted violently, injuring himself and his rider. The Brahman had to be put down, but not before throwing the rider and trampling him. The cowboy survived, but barely. Ended up with broken ribs, a shattered wrist, crushed pelvis and punctured spleen."

"So why wasn't Donahue arrested?"

"Not enough proof. No one saw him do it. He and his friends came up with an alibi." She glanced at Striker as he pulled into a parking space at Sharon's apartment building. "He never admitted drugging the bull, and I'm really not sure that it wasn't one of his buddies who actually did the injecting, but I'm sure that he was behind it. Just a gut feeling and the way he talked about the incident." She mentally chastised herself for being such a fool, and stared out the passenger window. "I'd already decided not to see him anymore and then, on top of all that, I discovered he was still married. Nice, huh?"

Striker cut the engine. "Not very."

"I know." The old pain cut deep, but she wasn't about to break down. Not in front of this man; not in front of anyone. Her jaw slid to one side. "Man, can I pick 'em."

Kurt touched her shoulder. "Just for the record, Randi. You deserve better than Donahue." She glanced his way and found him staring at her. His gaze scraped hers and beneath the hard facade, hidden in his eyes, a sliver of understanding, a tiny bit of empathy. "Come on. Let's go get your kid." He offered her the hint of a smile, then his grin faded quickly and the moment, that instant of connection, passed.

Her silly heart wrenched, and tears, so close to the surface, threatened.

She was out of the truck in a flash, taking the stairs to the upper-story unit two at a time. Suddenly frantic to see her baby, she pounded on the door. Sharon, a petite woman, answered. In her arms was Joshua. Blinking as if he'd just woken up from a nap, his fuzz of red-blond hair sticking straight up, he wiggled at the sight of her. Randi's heart split into a million pieces at the sight of her son. The tears she'd been fighting filled her eyes.

"Hey, big guy," she whispered, her voice hoarse.

"He missed you," Sharon said as she transferred the baby into Randi's hungry arms.

"Not half as bad as I missed him." Randi was snuggling her son, wrapped up in the wonder of holding him, smelling the baby shampoo in his hair and listening to the little coo that escaped those tiny lips, when she heard a quiet cough behind her. "Oh . . . this is Kurt Striker. Sharon Okano. Kurt is a friend of my brother Slade's." With an arch of her eyebrow, she added, "All of my brothers decided to hire him as, if you'll believe this, my personal bodyguard."

"Bodyguard?" Sharon's eyebrows lifted a bit. "How serious is this trouble you're in?"

"Serious enough, I guess. Kurt thinks it would be best if we kept the baby with us."

"Whatever you want." Sharon gently touched Joshua's cheek. "He's adorable, you know. I'm not sure that if you left him here much longer I could ever give him up."

"You need one of your own."

"But first, a man, I think," Sharon said. "They seem to be a necessary part of the equation." She glanced at Kurt, but Randi ignored the innuendo. She didn't need a man to help raise her son. She'd do just fine on her own.

They didn't stay long. While the women were packing Joshua's things, Kurt asked Sharon if she'd had any strange phone calls or visitors. When Sharon reported that nothing out of the ordinary had happened, Kurt called his partner and within fifteen minutes, Randi, Kurt and Joshua, tucked into his car seat, were on the road and heading east out of Seattle. The rain had started, a deep steady mist, and Striker had flipped on the wipers.

"You're still not going to tell me where we're going?" she asked.

"Inland."

"I know that much, but where exactly?" When he didn't immediately respond, she said, "I have a job to do. Remember? I can't be gone indefinitely." She glanced at her watch, scowled as it was after three, then dug in her purse, retrieved her cell phone and punched out the numbers for the

Clarion. Within a minute she was connected to Bill Withers's voice mail and left a quick message, indicating she had a family emergency and vowing she would e-mail a couple of new columns. As she hung up, she said, "I don't know how much of that Withers will buy, but it should give us a couple of days."

"Maybe that's all we'll need." He sped around a fuel truck, but his voice lacked conviction.

"Listen, Striker, we've got to nail this creep and soon," Randi said as the wipers slapped away the rain. "I need my life back."

The look he sent her sliced into her soul. "So do I."

The bitch wouldn't get away with it.

Three cars behind Striker's truck, gloved hands tight over the steering wheel, the would-be killer drove carefully, coming close to the pickup, then backing off, listening to a CD from the eighties as red taillights blurred. Jon Bon Jovi's voice wailed through the speakers and the stalker licked dry lips as the pickup cut across the floating bridge, over the steely waters of Lake Washington. Who knew where they were headed? To the suburbs of upscale Bellevue? Or somewhere around Lake Sammamish? Maybe farther into the forested hills. Even the Cascade Mountains.

Whatever.

It didn't matter.

Sweet vengeance brought a smile to the stalker's lips.

Randi McCafferty's destination was about to become her final resting place.

CHAPTER NINE

"Get the baby ready," Kurt said as he took an exit off the freeway. Glancing in the rearview mirror to be certain he wasn't followed, he doubled back, heading west, only to get off at the previous stop and drive along a frontage heading toward Seattle again.

"What are we doing?" Randi asked.

"Changing vehicles." Carefully he timed the stoplights, making certain he was the last vehicle through the two intersections before turning down one street and pulling into a gas station.

"What? Why?"

"I'm not taking any chances that we're being followed."

"You saw someone?"

"No."

"But —"

"Just make it fast and jump into that brown SUV." He nodded toward the back of the station to a banged-up vehicle with tinted windows and zero chrome. The SUV was completely nondescript, the fenders and tires splattered with mud. "It belongs to a friend of mine," Striker said. "He's waiting. He'll drive the truck."

"This is nuts," Randi muttered, but she unstrapped the baby seat and pulled it, along with Joshua, from the truck.

"I don't think so."

Quickly, as Randi did as she was told, Striker topped off his tank.

Eric was waiting for them. He'd been talking on his cell phone and smoking a cigarette, but spying Striker, tossed the cigarette into a puddle and gave a quick wave. Ending his call, he helped Randi load up, then traded places with Kurt. The entire exchange had taken less than a minute. Seconds after that, Kurt was in the driver's seat of the Jeep, heading east again.

"I don't think I can stand all of this cloak-and-dagger stuff," Randi complained, and even in the darkness he saw the outline of her jaw, the slope of her cheek, the purse of those incredible lips. Good Lord, she was one helluva woman. Intriguingly beautiful, sexy as hell, smarter than she needed to be and endowed with a tongue sharp enough to cut through a strong man's ego.

"Sure you can."

"Whatever my brothers are paying you, it's not enough."

"That's probably true." He glanced at her once more, then turned his attention to the road. Night had fallen, but the rain had let up a bit. His tires sang on the wet pavement and the rumble of the SUV's engine was smooth and steady. The baby was quiet in the back seat, and for the first time in years Kurt felt a little sensation of being with family. Which was ridiculous. The woman was a client, the child just part of the package. He told himself to remember that. No matter what else. He was her bodyguard. His job was to keep her alive and find out who was trying to kill her.

Nothing more.

What about the other night at the ranch? his damning mind taunted. *Remember how much you wanted her, how you went about seducing her? How can you forget the thrill of slipping her robe off her shoulders and unveiling those incredible breasts. What about the look of surprise and wonder in her eyes, or the soft, inviting curve of her lips as you kissed the hollow of her throat. Think about the raw need that drove you to untie the belt at her waist. The robe gave way, the nightgown followed and she was naked aside from a slim gold chain and locket at her throat. You didn't waste any time kicking off your jeans. You wanted her, Striker. More than you've ever wanted a woman in your life. You would have died to have her and you did, didn't you? Over and over again. Feeling her heat surround you, listening to the pounding of your heart and feeling your blood sing through your veins. You were so hot and hard, nothing could have stopped you. What about then, when you gave in to temptation?*

The back of his neck tightened as he remembered and his inner voice continued to taunt him.

If you can convince yourself that Randi Mc-Cafferty is just another client, then you're a bigger fool than you know.

It was late by the time the Jeep bounced along the rocky, mossy ruts that constituted the driveway to what could only be loosely called a cabin. Set deep in the forest and barricaded by a locked gate to which Kurt had miraculously had the key, the place was obviously deserted and had been for a long time. Randi shuddered inwardly as the Jeep's headlights illuminated the sorry little bungalow. Tattered shades were drawn over the windows, rust was evident in the few downspouts that were still connected to the gutters, and the moss-covered roof sagged pitifully.

"You sure you don't want to look for a Motel 6?" she asked. "Even a Motel 2 would be an improvement over this."

"Not yet." Kurt had already pulled on the emergency brake and cut the engine. "Think of it as rustic."

"Right. Rustic. And quaint." She shook her head.

"This used to be the gatekeeper's house when this area was actively being logged," he explained.

"And now?" She stepped out of the Jeep and her boots sank in the soggy loam of the forest floor.

"It's been a while since the cabin's been inhabited."

"A long while, I'd guess. Come on, baby, it's time to check out our new digs." She hauled Joshua in his carrier up creaky porch steps as Kurt, with the aid of a flashlight and another key, opened a door that creaked as it swung inward.

Kurt tried a light switch. Nothing. Just a loud click. "Juice isn't turned on, I guess."

"Fabulous."

He found a lantern and struck a match. Immediately the room was flooded with a soft golden glow that couldn't hide the dust, cobwebs and general malaise of the place. The floor was scarred fir, the ceiling pine was stained where rainwater had seeped inside and it smelled of must and years of neglect.

"Home sweet home," she cracked.

"For the time being." But Kurt was already stalking through the small rooms, running his flashlight along the floor and ceiling. "We won't have electricity, but we'll manage."

"So no hot water, light or heat."

"But a woodstove and lanterns. We'll be okay."

"What about a bathroom?"

He shook his head. "There's an old pump on the porch and, if you'll give me a minute —" he looked in a few cupboards and closets before coming up with a bucket "— voila! An old fashioned Porta Potti."

"Give me a break," she muttered.

"Come on, you're a McCafferty. Rustic living should be a piece of cake."

"Let me give you a clue, Striker. This is waaaay beyond rustic."

"I heard you were a tomboy growing up."

"Slade talks too much."

"Probably. But you used to camp all the time."

"In the summers. I was twelve or thirteen."

"It's like riding a bike. You never forget how."

"We'll see." But she didn't complain as they hauled in equipment that had been loaded into the Jeep. Sleeping bags, canned goods, a cooler for fresh food, cooking equipment, paper plates, propane stove, towels and toilet paper. "You thought this through."

"I just told Eric to pack the essentials."

"What about a phone?"

"Our cells should work."

Scrounging in her purse, she found her phone, yanked it out and turned it on. The backlit message wasn't encouraging. "Looking for service," she read aloud, and watched as the cell failed to find a signal. "Hopefully yours is stronger."

He flashed her a grin that seemed to sizzle in the dim light. "I already checked. It works."

"So what about a phone jack to link up my laptop?"

He lifted a shoulder. "Looks like you're out of luck unless you've got one of those wireless hookups."

"Not a prayer."

"Then you'll have to be out of touch for a while."

"Great," she muttered. "I don't suppose it

matters that I could lose my job over this."

"Better than your life."

She was about to reply, when the baby began to cry. Quickly, Randi mixed formula with some of the bottled water she'd brought, then pulled off dust cloths from furniture that looked as if it was in style around the end of World War II. Joshua was really cranking it up by the time Randi plopped herself into a rocking chair and braced herself for the sound of scurrying feet as mice skittered out from the old cushions. Fortunately, as she settled into the chair, no protesting squeaks erupted, nor did any little scurrying rodent make a mad dash to the darker corners. With the baby's blanket wrapped around him, she fed her son and felt a few seconds' relaxation as his wails subsided and he ate hungrily from the bottle. There was a peace to holding her baby, a calm that kept her fears and worries at bay. He looked up at her as he ate, and in those precious, bonding moments, she never once doubted that her affair with Sam Donahue was worth every second of her later regrets.

Kurt was busy checking the flue, starting a fire in an antique-looking woodstove. Once the fire was crackling, he rocked back on his heels and dusted his hands. She tried not to notice how his jacket stretched at the shoulders or the way his jeans fit snug around his hips and buttocks. Nor did she want to observe that his hair fell in an unruly lock over his forehead, or that his cheekbones were strong enough to hint at some long-forgotten Native American heritage.

He was too damn sexy for his own good.

As if sensing her watching him, he straightened slowly and she was given a bird's-eye view of his long back as he stretched, then walked to a black beat-up leather case and unzipped it. Out came a laptop computer complete with wireless connection device.

He glanced over his shoulder, his green eyes glinting in amusement.

"You could have said something," she charged.

"And miss seeing you get ticked off? No way. But this isn't the be-all and end-all. I have one extra battery. No more. Since there's no electricity here, the juice won't last forever."

"Wonderful," she said, lifting her baby to her shoulder and gently rubbing his back.

"It's better than nothing."

"Can I use it?"

"For a small fee," he said as the corners

of his mouth twitched.

"You are *so* full of it."

"Wouldn't want to disappoint."

"You never do, Striker."

"Good. Let's keep it that way."

Joshua gave a loud burp. "There we go, big guy," she whispered as she spread his blanket on a pad and changed his diaper. The baby kicked and gurgled, his eyes bright in the firelight. "Oh, you're full of the devil, aren't you?" She played with him a few more minutes until he yawned and sighed. Randi held him and swayed a little as he nodded off. She couldn't imagine what life would have been like without this precious little boy. She kissed his soft crown, and as his breathing became regular and his head heavy, she placed him upon the make-shift crib of blankets and pillows, then glanced around the stark, near-empty cabin. "We really are in the middle of no-darned-where."

"That was the general idea."

She ran a finger through the dust on an old scarred table. "No electricity, no indoor plumbing, no television, radio or even any good books lying around."

"I guess we'll just have to make do and find some way to amuse ourselves." His expression was positively wicked, his eyes glittering with amusement. That he could find even the tiniest bit of humor in this vile situation was something, she thought, though she didn't like the way her throat caught when he stared at her, nor the way blood went rushing through her veins as he cocked an arrogant eyebrow.

"I think we'll do just fine," she said, hoping to sound frosty when, in fact, her voice was more than a tad breathless. Damn it all, she didn't like the idea of being trapped here with him in the middle of God-only-knew-where, didn't like feeling vulnerable not only to whoever was stalking her, but also to the warring emotions she felt whenever she was around Striker. *Don't even go there,* she told herself. *All you have to do is get through the next few days. By then, if he does his job the way he's supposed to, he'll catch the bad guy and you can reclaim your life. Then, you'll be safe. You and your baby can start over.*

Unless something goes wrong. Terribly, terribly wrong.

She glanced again at Striker.

Whether she liked it or not, she was stuck with him.

Things could be worse.

Less than two hours later, Striker's phone jangled.

He jumped and snapped it open. "Striker."

"It's Kelly. I've got information."

Finally! He leaned a hip against an old windowsill and watched as Randi, glasses perched on the end of her nose, looked up from his laptop. "News?"

He nodded. "Go on," he said into the phone and listened as Matt McCafferty's wife began to explain.

"I think I've located the vehicle that forced Randi off the road in Glacier Park. A maroon Ford truck, a few years old, had some dents banged out of it in a chop shop in Idaho. All under-the-table stuff. Got the lead from a disgruntled employee who swears the chop shop owner owes him back wages."

Striker's jaw hardened. "Let me guess. The truck was registered to Sam Donahue."

"Close. Actually was once owned by Marv Bates, or, precisely, a girlfriend of his."

"Have you located Bates?"

Randi visibly stiffened. She set aside the laptop and crossed the few feet separating them. "We're working on it. I've got the police involved. My old boss, Espinoza, is doing what he can." Roberto Espinoza was a senior detective who was working on Randi's case. Kelly Dillinger had once worked for him, but turned in her badge about the time she married Matt McCafferty. "But so far, we haven't been able to locate Mr. Bates."

"He had an alibi."

"Yeah," Kelly said. "Airtight. Good ol' boys Sam Donahue and Charlie Caldwell swore they were all over at Marv's house when Randi was forced off the road. Charlie's girlfriend at the time, Trina Spencer, verified the story, but now Charlie and Trina have split, so we're looking for her. Maybe she'll change her tune now that Charlie's no longer the love of her life and the truck she owned has been linked to the crime. We're talking to the employees of the chop shop. I figure it's just a matter of time before one of 'em cracks."

"Good. It's a start."

"Finally," Kelly agreed. "I'll keep working on it."

"Want to talk to Randi?"

"Absolutely." Striker handed the phone to Randi and listened to her end of the conversation as she asked about what Kelly had discovered, then turned the conversation to her family. A few minutes later, she hung up.

"This is the break you've been waiting for," she said, and he heard the hope in her voice.

God, he hated to burst her bubble. "It's a start, Randi. Time will tell if it pans out, but yeah, it's something."

He only hoped it was enough.

"Why don't you turn in." He unrolled a sleeping bag, placing it between the baby's makeshift crib and the fire.

"Where will you be?"

"Here." He shoved a chair close to the door.

She eyed the old wingback. "Aren't you going to sleep?"

"Maybe doze."

"You're still afraid," she charged.

"Not afraid. Just vigilant."

She shook her head, unaware that the fire's glow brought out the red streaks in her hair. Sighing, she started working off one boot with the toe of another. "I really can't believe this is my life." The first boot came off, followed quickly by the second. Plopping down on the sleeping bag, she sat cross-legged and stared at the fire. "I just wanted to write a book, you know. Show my dad, my boss, even my brothers that I was capable of doing something really newsworthy. My family thought I was nuts when I went into journalism in college — my dad in particular. He couldn't see any use in it. Not for his daughter, anyway. And then I landed the job with the paper in Seattle and it became a joke. Advice to single people. My brothers thought it was just a lot of fluff, even when the column took off and was syndicated." She glanced at Striker. "You know my brothers. They're pretty much straight-shooter, feet-on-the-ground types. I don't think Matt or Slade or Thorne would ever be ones to write in for advice on their love lives."

Kurt laughed.

"Nor you, I suppose?"

He arched an eyebrow in her direction. "Not likely."

"And the articles I did for magazines under R. J. McKay, it was all woman stuff, too. So the book —" she looked up at the ceiling as if she could find an answer in the cobwebby beams and rafters "— it was an attempt to legitimatize my career. Unfortunately Dad died before it was finished and then all the trouble started." She rubbed her knees and cocked her head. Her locket slipped over the collar of her shirt and he noticed it winking in the firelight. His mouth turned dry at the sight of her slim throat and the curve of her neck where it met her shoulder. A tightening in his groin forced him to look away.

"Maybe the trouble's about to end."

"That would be heaven," she said. "You know, I always liked living on the edge, being a part of the action, whatever it was, never set my roots down too deep."

"A true McCafferty."

She chuckled. "I suppose. But now, with the baby and after everything that happened, I just want some peace of mind. I want my life in the city back."

"And the book?"

Her smile grew slowly. "Oh, I'm still going to write it," she vowed, and he noticed a determined edge to her voice, a steely resolve hidden in her grin. "Bedtime?"

The question sounded innocent, but it still created an image of their lovemaking. "Whenever you want."

"And you're just going to play security guard by the door."

"Yep." He nodded. "Get some sleep."

"Not until you tell me what it is that makes you tick," she said. "Come on, I told you all about my dreams of being a journalist and how my family practically laughed in my face. You know all about the men I've dated in recent history and I've also told you about my book and how I got involved with a man who was still married and might be trying to kill me. Whatever you're hiding can't be that bad."

"Why do you think I'm hiding something?"

"We all have secrets, Striker. What's yours?"

That I'm falling for you, he thought, then clamped his mind shut. No way. No how. His involvement with Randi McCafferty had to remain professional. No matter what. "I was married," he said, and felt that old raw pain cutting through him.

"What happened?"

He hesitated. This was a subject he rarely bridged, never brought up on his own. "She divorced me."

"Because of your work?"

"No." He glanced at her baby sleeping so soundly in his blankets, remembered the rush of seeing his own child for the first time, remembered the smell of her, the wonder of caring too much for one little beguiling person.

"Another woman?" she asked, and he saw the wariness in the set of her jaw.

"No. That would have been easier," he admitted. "Cleaner."

170

"Then, what happened? Don't give me any of that 'we grew away from each other' or 'we drifted apart.' I have readers who write me by the dozens and they all say the same thing."

"What happened between me and my ex-wife can't be cured by advice in your column," he said more bitterly than he'd planned.

"I didn't mean to imply that it could." She was a little angry. He could feel it.

"Good."

"So what happened, Striker?"

His jaw worked.

"Can't talk about it?" She rolled her eyes. "After I explained about Sam Donahue? That I was sleeping with him and he was still married. How do you think I feel, not seeing the signs, not reading the clues. Geez, whatever it is can't be that humiliating!"

"We had a daughter," he said, his voice seeming to come from outside his body. "Her name was Heather." His throat tightened with the memories. "I used to take her with me on the boat and she loved it. My wife didn't like it, was afraid of the water. But I insisted it would be safe. And it was. Until . . ." His chest felt as if the weight of the sea was upon it. Randi didn't say a word but she'd blanched, her skin suddenly pale, as if she knew what was to come. Striker closed his eyes, but still he could see that day, the storm coming in on the horizon, remember the way the engine had stalled. "Until the last time. Heather and I went boating. The engine had cut out and I was busy fiddling with it when she fell overboard. Somehow her life jacket slipped off. It was a fluke, but still . . . I dived in after her but she'd struck her head. Took in too much water." He blinked hard. "It was too late. I couldn't save her." Pain wracked through his soul.

Randi didn't move. Just stared at him.

"My wife blamed me," he said, leaning against the door. "The divorce was just a formality."

CHAPTER TEN

Dear God, how she'd misjudged him! "I'm so sorry," she whispered, wondering how anyone survived losing a child.

"It's not your fault."

"And it wasn't yours. It was an accident," she said then saw recrimination darken his gaze.

"So I told myself. But if I hadn't insisted upon taking her . . ." He scowled. "Look, it happened. Over five years ago. No reason to bring it up now."

Randi's heart split. For all of his denials, the pain was fresh in him. "Do you have a picture?"

"What?"

"Of your daughter?"

When he hesitated, she crawled out of the sleeping bag. "I'd like to see."

"This isn't a good idea."

"Not the first," she said as she crossed the room. Reluctantly he reached into his back pocket, pulled out his wallet and flipped it open. Randi's throat closed as she took the battered leather and gazed at the plastic-encased photograph of a darling little girl. Blond pigtails framed a cherubic face that seemed primed for the camera's eye. Under apple cheeks, her tiny grin showed off perfect little baby teeth. "She's beautiful."

"Yes." He nodded, his lips thin and tight. "She was."

"I apologize if I said anything insensitive before. I didn't know."

"I don't talk about it much."

"Maybe you should."

"Don't think so." He took the wallet from her fingers and snapped it shut.

"If I'd known . . ."

"What? What would you have done differently?" he asked, a trace of bitterness to his words. "There's nothing you can say, nothing you can do, nothing that will change what happened."

She reached forward to stroke his cheek and he grabbed her wrist. "Don't," he warned. "I don't want your pity or your sympathy."

"Empathy," she said.

"No one who hasn't lost a child can empathize," he said, his fingers tightening, his eyes fierce. "It's just not possible."

"Maybe not, but that doesn't mean I can't feel some of your pain."

"Well, don't. It's mine. You can do nothing." A muscle worked in his jaw. "I shouldn't have told you."

"No . . . it's better."

"How?" he demanded, his nostrils flaring. "Tell me how you knowing about Heather helps anything."

"I understand you better."

"Jesus, Randi. That's woman patter. You don't need to figure out what makes me tick or even know about what I've been through. You weren't there, okay? So I'd rather you not try to 'feel my pain' or any of that self-aggrandizing pseudopsychological, television talk-show crap. You just need to do what I tell you to do so that we can make certain that you and your son are safe. End of story."

"Not quite," she whispered, and without thinking, placed a kiss on the corner of his mouth. The need to soothe him was overpowering, nearly as intense as her own need to be comforted. To be held. "If we're going to be sequestered from the rest of the world, I do need to understand you." She kissed him again.

"Don't do that." His voice was hoarse and she noticed that he shifted, as if his jeans were suddenly too tight.

"Why?" she asked, not budging an inch, so close she smelled the rain drying on his jacket. She felt reckless and wild and wanted to touch him and hold him close, this man who had seen so much of life, felt so much pain.

"You know why."

"Kurt, I just want to help."

"You can't." He turned to look her square in the eye, his nose only inches from hers. "Don't you know what you're dealing with here?"

"I'm not afraid." She kissed his cheek and he groaned.

"Don't do this, Randi," he ordered, but it sounded like a plea.

"You can trust me."

"This isn't about trust."

"No? Then why are we here? Alone together? If I didn't trust you, you can bet I wouldn't be locked away from the world like this. Believe me, Striker, this is all about trust. That's why you told me about Heather."

"Let's leave her out of this!" he growled.

"You have a right to be angry about what happened to your daughter."

"Good. 'Cuz I am and you're not helping!"

"No?" she said, her temper snapping. "Then I don't suppose I helped the other night, either?"

"Hell," he muttered, glancing away. His fingers were still surrounding her wrist, her pulse beating wildly beneath the warm pads.

"You remember that night, don't you?" she reminded him. "The one where you were watching me from the second story? *That* night, you didn't have any of these reservations."

"That night is the reason I'm having these reservations. It was a mistake."

"You didn't think so at the time."

"You're right, I didn't think period. But I'm trying to now."

"So it's okay for you to seduce me, but not the other way around."

He closed his eyes as if to gain strength. "I didn't bring you up here to sleep with you."

"No?" She kissed him again, behind his ear, and this time his reaction was immediate.

He turned swiftly, pinning her onto the floor and leaning over her. "Look, woman, you're pushing it with me. A man can only take so much."

"Same with a woman," she said. "You can't just —"

The rest of her sentence was cut off as his lips clamped over hers. Fierce. Hot. Hard. Desperate. He kissed her long and wildly and she responded, opening her mouth, feeling his tongue slide into her, arching as it probed. Her breath was trapped, her blood on fire, her bones melting as he slid his hands up and down her body. No longer did he deny what they both wanted. No longer did he say a word, just kissed and touched and tugged at her clothes.

She had no regrets. This was what she wanted. To touch him, physically and emotionally. Her own fingers struggled with the zipper of his coat and the shirt buttons below. She felt strong sinewy muscles covered by taut skin and chest hair that was stiff. Her fingertips grazed nipples that tightened at her touch.

"Oh, God," he rasped as he yanked off his shirt, then worked at the hem of her sweater. Strong, callused hands rubbed her skin as he scaled her ribs. She cried out as he touched beneath her bra, skimming the underside of her breasts. Her nipples tightened. Her breasts filled and she wanted him. With every breath in her body, she needed to feel him inside her, to have him rubbing and moving and balming the ache growing deep within. He peeled away her bra and scooped her into his strong arms, climbed to his feet and carried her to the sleeping bag, where they fell into a tangle of arms and legs. His mouth was ravenous as he kissed her face and breasts. Hard fingers splayed against the small of her back, pulling her tight against him, pressing her mound into the hardness of his fly, rubbing her sensually.

She moaned softly as he kissed her nipples, teasing them with his tongue and lips, biting softly before he nuzzled and sucked. Her mind spun in dizzying fragments of light and shadow. She saw his face buried into her breasts, felt his fingertips probing beneath the waistband of her pants, burned with a want so hot she was sweating in the cold room, aching for him, her fingers reaching for his fly. "Randi," he whispered across her wet breasts. "Oh, God, darlin' . . ." His hand slid down the slope of her rump, fingers stretching to find that sweet spot within her. She cried out and moved her hips as he yanked off her pants with his free hand and continued to explore with his other. Parting her. Delving deep. Causing her to gasp and throw her head back as she arched and he suckled at her breast. He scratched the surface of her need. Liquid warmth seared her.

"More," she whispered, lost.

He stripped her panties from her.

She fumbled with the buttons of his fly, but they came undone and, with amazing agility, he kicked out of his jeans to be naked with her. Skin on skin. Flesh on flesh. Blood heating, he pulled her atop him, and in one quick movement removed his hand and replaced it with his thick, hard erection.

"Oh!" she cried as he pushed her hips down and raised his buttocks in one swift motion. The world melted away as they began to move. Slowly at first. Friction and fire. Heat and want. All emotion and need. Randi closed her eyes and heard a slow, long moan. From her throat or his? She didn't know, didn't care. Nothing mattered but the man beneath her, the man she wanted, the man she feared she loved. This small moment in time could very well be their last, but she didn't care, just wanted to feel him within her.

Deep inside something snapped. She wanted more of him. More. So much more. Opening her eyes, she saw him staring at her, his own gaze bright with the same desire as her own. "That's it, baby," he whispered as she increased the tempo. He caught up quickly and took command, his hands tight on her as he began pumping furiously beneath her. Beads of sweat dotted his forehead, his skin tight, his hair damp with perspiration. Yet he didn't stop.

Hotter. Faster. The world spinning. "Oh, God, oh, God, oh . . . oh . . ." she cried as the world seemed to catch fire and explode around her. She convulsed, but still he held her upright, still he thrust into her, and though she'd felt complete surrender a minute before, she met each of his jabs with her own downward motion. Again. And again . . . Over and over until the heat rose in her in such a rush that she bucked. This time he came with her, his breath screaming out of his lungs, his body straining upward as he let go and finally emptied himself into her.

"Randi!" he cried hoarsely, his voice breaking, "Oh, love . . ."

She fell against him and felt his strong arms surround her and hold her close. One hand cradled her head, the other was wrapped around her waist. Tears sprang unbidden to her eyes as his words echoed through her head. Though they were spoken in the throes of passion, though she knew she would never hear them again, she clung to them. Randi . . . Oh, love.

They would be meaningless in the morning, but for now, for all of this night, they sustained her. She cuddled up against him, and knew a few moments' peace. For tonight, she would indulge herself. For tonight, she would sleep with this man she could so easily love. For tonight she'd forget that he was her bodyguard, paid to protect her, a man who no woman in her right mind would allow herself to fall for.

Lovers.

She and Kurt had become lovers.

The thought hit her hard, battering at her before she opened her eyes and knew that he wasn't in the sleeping bag with her. They'd made love over and over the night before and now . . . She opened one eye to the cabin as morning light streamed through the dusty windows. If anything, the dilapidated old cottage looked worse in the gloom of the day. The baby was rustling. It had probably been his soft cries that had cut through her thick slumber and roused her. So here she was, naked, cold, no sign of Kurt, in the middle of nowhere.

"Coming," she called to the baby as she found her clothes and slid into them. As she felt a slight soreness between her legs, a reminder of what had happened, what she'd instigated last night. What had she been thinking? Embarrassed at her actions, she crawled over to her baby and smiled down at his beatific face. "Hungry?" she asked, though she was already changing him. How quickly she'd become adept at holding him in place, talking to him, removing the old diaper, cleaning him and whipping a new diaper around him.

She found premixed formula in a bottle and, singing softly, fed her child. She heard the door open and looked over her shoulder to spy Kurt, carrying an armload of split kindling into the cabin. She felt heat wash up the back of her neck, but he didn't seem embarrassed. "Mornin'," he drawled, and the look he sent her reminded her of their lovemaking all over again. She'd been the aggressor. She'd practically begged him to make love to her. She'd definitely seduced him and now she felt the fool.

"I think I should say something about last night," she offered.

"What's to say?"

"That I'm not usually like that . . ."

"Too bad." One side of his mouth lifted. "I thought it was pretty damn nice."

"Really? But you . . . I mean you acted like it was a mistake. You *said* it was one."

"But it happened, right? I think we shouldn't second-guess ourselves."

"So it was no big deal?" she asked, and felt slightly deflated.

"It was a big deal, but let's not start the morning with recriminations, okay? I don't think that would solve anything. As I said, I'm not into overanalyzing emotions." He stacked the kindling in an old crate that was probably home to several nests of spiders. "I was hoping to make coffee before you woke up."

"Mmm. Sounds like heaven," she admitted.

"It'll be just a second." He dusted his hands and found a packet of coffee.

"I don't suppose you have a nonfat, vanilla latte with extra foam and chocolate sprinkles?" she asked, and he snorted a laugh.

"You lived in Seattle too long."

"Tell that to my boss," she muttered. "Actually, when I'm finished here . . ." She inclined her head toward her son. "I want to call him. If I'm allowed," she added.

"Just as long as you don't divulge our whereabouts."

"That would be tough considering that I don't know where we are." Randi finished feeding the baby and played with him as she changed his clothes. While Kurt heated water for the instant coffee, she balanced her son to her shoulder and put in another call to Bill Withers, only to leave another voice message when the editor didn't pick up his phone. "Withers must be ducking me," she muttered as she redialed and connected with Sarah.

"Where've you been?" Sarah demanded once she realized she was talking to Randi. "Bill gave me the third degree, and whenever your name is mentioned, he looks as if he's having a seizure."

"I can't really say, but I'll be back —" she glanced at Kurt who was shaking his head "— soon. I don't really know when. In the meantime I'm going to e-mail my stories. It shouldn't be that big of a deal, most of the questions I get come in over the Internet."

"It's a control issue with Bill, but then it is with most men."

"Especially if the man happens to be your boss," Randi said. "Look, if he talks to you, tell him I'm trying to get hold of him. I've called twice and I'm going to e-mail in a couple of hours."

"Well, hurry back, okay?"

"I'll be back as soon as I can," Randi assured her.

"Should I tell Joe?"

"What?"

"Paterno's back in town and he's been

asking about you."

Randi and Joe had never been lovers, their relationship hadn't blossomed in a romantic way. She was surprised that he'd be looking for her. "Well, tell him I'll get back to him when I'm in town," she said, and saw Striker stiffen slightly. He couldn't help but overhear her conversation and she didn't like the fact that she had so little privacy. "Look, Sarah, I've got to run." She hung up, hoping to save as much battery as possible before Sarah could argue. Exchanging the phone for a cup of coffee, she said, "So I didn't lie, did I? This will end soon."

"I think so, but I did some checking this morning before you woke and so far no one's been able to locate Sam Donahue."

"You think he's hiding?"

"Maybe."

"Or . . . ?" She didn't like the feeling she was getting. "Or you think he's followed us?"

"I don't know. Did he come looking for you at the office? I heard you tell your friend that you'd get back with him."

"That wasn't Sam." She hesitated, then decided to come clean. "It was Joe Paterno. We were . . . are . . . friends. That's all. That's all there ever was between us."

He looked as if he didn't believe her.

"Really." She lifted a shoulder. "Sorry to disappoint you. I get the feeling that you think I had this incredible love life, that I slept with every man I dated, but that just wasn't the case. I let everyone wonder about my baby's paternity to protect him. The fewer people who knew that Sam was the baby's father, the better it was for me and Joshua. At least that's what I thought, so I let people draw their own conclusions about my love life." She arched an eyebrow at him. "I might not have the best taste in men, but I am somewhat picky."

"I guess I should feel flattered."

"Damn straight," she said, sending a look guaranteed to kill, then took a long swallow of coffee before turning her attention to her baby. After all, he was the reason that everything was happening and Randi wouldn't have changed a thing. Not if it meant she never would have had her son. Joshua made it all worthwhile.

Even the accident, she thought as the baby giggled and cooed.

Late last fall she'd left Seattle intending to return to the ranch she'd inherited from her father. She'd just wanted some peace of mind and time alone in Montana where she intended to write her book and do some serious soul-searching. Once on the ranch, she'd made some stupid mistakes including firing Larry Todd, the foreman, and even letting Juanita Ramirez, the housekeeper, go. Those decisions had been stupid, as Larry had known the livestock backward and forward and Juanita had not only helped raise Randi and her half brothers but had put up with their father until the grumpy old man had died. But Randi had been on a mission and had believed that before she could take care of a baby, she had to prove to herself that she could be completely self-reliant.

She'd thought that living on the Flying M, returning to her roots and running the ranch while writing her book might be the right kind of therapy she needed. After the baby came, she'd figured she could look after her child and raise him where she'd grown up, away from the hustle and bustle of the city. Plus, she still had her job at the *Clarion,* using e-mail and a fax machine, until she could return to Seattle every other week or so if need be.

The prospect of becoming a mother — a single mother — had been daunting. How would she deal with her son's inevitable questions about his father? When she finished the book and the scam was exposed, many people in the rodeo world, including

Sam Donahue, would be investigated and possibly indicted. How would she feel knowing that she'd sent her son's father to prison?

Nevertheless, because she'd been born a McCafferty, the kind of person who never shied away from the truth or tough decisions, she'd come to the conclusion that she had to let the truth be known and let the chips fall where they may.

But she hadn't gotten the chance. On her way back to Grand Hope, she'd had the accident that had nearly taken her life and sent her into premature labor. She'd been laid up in a coma, woken up to find out that she couldn't remember anything and that she had this wonderful infant son. As she'd recovered and her memory had returned in bits and snatches, she was horrified to realize that she'd been played for a fool, that Sam Donahue was Joshua's father and that he was a heartless criminal.

And now . . . *And now what?* She leaned closer to the baby and her locket swung free of her shirt. Joshua giggled and smiled, kicking and reaching for the glittering gold heart. "Silly boy," she said, leaning over to buss him in the tummy. He chortled and she did it again, making a game of it, closing out her doubts and worries as she played with her child.

Striker's cell phone rang, disturbing the quiet.

He flipped it open and answered, "Kurt Striker . . . Yeah, she's right here . . . I don't know if that's such a great idea. . . . Fine. Just a sec."

Randi turned her head and saw Striker glowering through the window, his cell phone pressed against his ear. He glanced her way and her heart nearly stopped. Something had happened. Something bad. "What?"

"Okay, put him on, but I don't have much battery left, so he'd better keep it short." He held the phone toward Randi. "That was Brown. He found Sam Donahue."

The floor seemed to wobble. "And?"

"It's for you, darlin'." Kurt's smile was cold as ice. "Seems as if good ol' Sam wants to talk to you."

CHAPTER ELEVEN

"What the hell's going on, Randi?" Sam Donahue shouted through the phone wires.

Randi braced herself for the onslaught. And it came.

"I've got some crazy son of a bitch telling me that I'm gonna be arrested because I tried to kill you or some damn thing and that's all a pile of crap. You *know* it's crap. Why would I want to hurt you? Because of the kid? Oh, give me a break! That story you're writing? Who would believe it? I've got an ironclad alibi, so call off your dogs!"

"My dogs?" she repeated as static crackled in her ear. The signal was fading and fast. Thankfully.

"Yeah, this guy. Brown."

"I can't hear you, Sam."

". . . nuts! Crazy! He's talkin' about the police . . . Oh, God, they're here . . . Look, Randi, I don't know what this is all about, maybe some personal vendetta or something

. . . This is all wrong," he said, swearing a blue streak that broke up as the battery in the phone began to give out. ". . . damn it . . . sue you and anyone . . . false arrest . . . no way . . . Leave me the hell alone! Wait . . . Randi . . ." His voice faded completely and the connection stopped just as the cell phone beeped a final warning about its battery running low.

Numbly, she handed the phone back to Striker.

"What did he want?"

"To protest his innocence," she said. "He told me to call off my dogs."

"They aren't yours."

"I didn't have time to explain. He didn't give me much of a chance and the connection was miserable." She shoved her hands into the pockets of her jeans. "Not that I wanted to straighten him out." She glanced at her baby, sleeping again, so angelic, so unaware.

"You okay?" Kurt asked, rubbing the back of her neck in that comforting spot between her shoulder blades.

"Yeah. It wasn't all that emotional for me. I was surprised." She managed a sad smile. "You know, I thought I'd feel something. Anger, maybe, or even wistfulness, *any* kind of emotion because he *is* the father of my child, but I just felt . . . empty. And maybe a little sad. Not for me, but for Joshua." She shrugged. "Hard to explain." She glanced around the cabin, her gaze landing on her baby, who despite the tense conversation had fallen asleep. "But the odd thing about the phone call was that I believed him."

"Donahue?" Striker snorted as he walked to the fire and warmed his hands.

"Yes. I mean, he was so vehement, so outraged that he was being arrested. It didn't seem like an act."

Striker barked out a laugh. "You thought he'd go quietly?"

"No, of course not, but —"

"You're still protecting him," Kurt said with a frown. "You know, just because he's the father of your child doesn't mean you owe him any allegiance or anything."

That stung. "Are you kidding? The last thing I feel for Sam Donahue is allegiance. He was married when he and I met. *Married.* Not just going with someone, or even engaged. When I asked him about it, he'd said he was divorced, that they'd been separated for some time and the divorce had been final for months. He flat-out lied. Silly me. I believed him," she admitted, but that old pain, the embarrassment of falling for Donahue's line and lies wasn't as deep.

She'd fantasized about meeting or talking with him again, of either telling him to go to hell or advising him that he had a son who was the most precious thing on earth. And she'd hoped to feel some satisfaction in the conversation, but instead, all she'd felt was relief that she wasn't involved with him, that she was here, with Kurt Striker, that in fact, she'd moved on.

To what? A man who has been up front about his need to be independent; a sexy, single man who had no intention of settling down; a man who was so hurt after losing his child that he's formed a wall around his heart that no sane woman would try to scale. He's your bodyguard, Randi. Bought and paid for by your brothers. Don't be stupid enough to throw love into the mix. You'll only get hurt if you do.

Kurt added a chunk of wood to the fire. The mossy fir sizzled and popped. "And still you believe him. Defend him."

"That's not what I was doing. I was just . . . I mean, if he's guilty, okay. But . . . I still believe in innocent until proven guilty. That's the law, isn't it?"

"Right. That's the law. I'll just have to prove that he's the culprit."

"If you can."

A muscle jumped in Striker's jaw as he

glanced over his shoulder. "Watch me." He swung the door of the woodstove shut so hard it banged, and Joshua, startled, let up a little cry.

Randi shot across the room and scooped up her baby. "It's all right," she whispered, holding him close and kissing a downy-soft cheek. But Joshua was already revving up — his cries, originally whimpers, grew louder, and his nose was beginning to run.

Striker looked at the baby and an expression of regret darkened his gaze. "I'll go see if I can recharge the cell's battery in the truck. I've got a second phone, but it doesn't hold a charge worth crap." With that he was out the door, letting in a gust of damp, cool air before the door slammed shut behind him.

"Battery, my eye," Randi confided to her tousle-haired son. "He just wants to put a little space between us." Which was fine. She needed time to think about the complications that had become her life and to hold her child. What was it about Striker that got to her? It seemed that they were always making either love or war. With Kurt, her passions ran white hot and ice cold. There was nothing in between. And her emotions were always raw, her nerves strung taut whenever she was around him.

*Because you're falling in love with him, you
idiot. Don't you see? Even now you're sneak-
ing peeks out the window, hoping to catch a
glimpse of him. You've got it bad, Randi. Real
bad. If you don't watch out, Kurt Striker is going to break your heart.*

From a van near Eric Brown's apartment,
the would-be killer hung up the phone and
didn't bother smothering a smile. High tech
was just so damn great. All one needed to
know was how to tap into a cellular call,
and that was pretty basic stuff these days.
Easy as pie.

A fine mist had collected on the windshield and traffic, wheels humming against
the wet pavement, spun by the parking lot
of the convenience store where the van was
parked. No one looked twice at the dark
vehicle with its tinted windows. No one
cared. Which made things so much easier.

Taking out a map, the stalker studied the
roads and terrain of central Washington. So
the bitch and her lover were in the mountains. With the kid. Hiding out like scared
puppies. Which was fine and dandy. It
wouldn't take long to flush her out and
watch her run. The only question was,
which way would Randi McCafferty flee?

To her condo on the lake?

Or back to Daddy's ranch and that herd of tough-as-nails brothers?

West?

Or east?

It didn't matter. What was the old saying? Patience was a virtue. Yeah, well, probably overrated, but there was another adage . . . Revenge is best served up cold.

Hmmph. Cold or hot, it didn't matter. Just as long as vengeance was served.

And it would be. No doubt about it.

The baby was fussy as if he, too, could feel the charged atmosphere between Randi and Kurt.

Randi changed Joshua's diaper and gave up on the column she'd been composing on Striker's computer. The article would have to wait. Until her son was calmer. Quieter.

Joshua had been out of sorts for two days now and Randi didn't blame him. Being here, trapped with Kurt Striker, was driving her crazy. It was little wonder her baby had picked up on the emotional pressure. But Randi was afraid there was more to the baby's cries than his just being out of sorts.

Joshua was usually a happy infant but now he cried almost constantly. Nothing would calm him until he fell asleep. His face seemed rosier than usual and his nose ran a bit. Randi checked his temperature and it was up a degree, so she was watching her child with an eagle eye and trying like crazy not to panic. She could deal with this. She was his mother. Okay, so she was a *new* mother, but some things are instinctive, right? She should know what to do. Women raised babies all the time, married women, single women, rich women, poor women. Surely there wasn't a secret that had somehow, through the ages, been cosmically and genetically denied to her and her alone. No way. She could deal with a little runny nose, a slight fever, the hint of a cough. She was Joshua's mother, for God's sake.

While trying to convince herself of her maternal infallibility, she wrapped Joshua in blankets, held him whenever she could, prayed that he'd snap out of it and generally worried that she was doing everything wrong.

"If he doesn't get better, I want to take him to a pediatrician," she told Kurt on the third day.

"You think something's wrong?" Striker had just finished stoking the fire and was obviously frustrated that he'd not heard back from the police or Eric Brown.

"I just want to make certain that he's okay."

"I don't think we can leave just yet." Striker walked over to the baby. With amazing gentleness, he plucked Joshua out of Randi's arms and, squatting, cradled Randi's son as if he'd done it all his life. "How're ya doin', sport?" he asked, and the baby blinked, then blew bubbles with his tiny lips. With a smile so tender it touched Randi's heart, Striker glanced up at her. "Seems fine to me."

"But he's been fussy."

"Must take after his mother."

"His temperature is running a little hot."

He crooked an eyebrow and his gaze raked her from her feet to her chest, where he stopped, pointedly, then finally looked into her eyes.

"Say it and die," she warned.

"Wouldn't dare, lady. You've got me runnin' scared." He handed Joshua back to her.

"Very funny." She pretended to be angry, though she couldn't help but smile. "Okay, okay, so maybe I'm overreacting."

"Give the kid a chance. He might have a little cold, but we'll keep an eye on it."

"Easy for you to say. You're not a parent . . ." She let her voice fade as she saw Striker flinch. "Oh, God, I'm sorry," she whispered, wishing she could take back the thoughtless comment. But it was too late. The damage had been done. No doubt Kurt was reminded of the day he'd lost his own precious daughter.

"Just watch him," Striker advised, then walked outside.

Randi mentally kicked herself from one side of the cabin to the other. She thought about running after him, but decided against it. No . . . they all needed a little space. She thought of her condo in Seattle. If she were there . . . then what would she do? She'd be alone and have to leave Joshua with a babysitter.

Yeah, a professional. Someone who probably understands crying, fussy babies with runny noses a helluva lot better than you.

But the thought wasn't calming

And there still was the issue of someone having been inside her place. Someone having a key. The more she considered it, the more convinced she was that someone had broken in — or just walked in — and made himself at home. A shiver ran across the nape of Randi's neck. The thought of someone being so bold, so arrogant, so damn intrusive bothered her. Of course, she could change the locks, but she couldn't change the fact that she and the baby were alone in a city of strangers. Yes, she had a few friends, but who could she really depend upon?

She glanced at the window and saw Kurt striding to his truck. Tall. Rangy. Tough as nails, but with a kinder, more human side as well. Sunlight caught against his bare head, glinting the lighter brown strands gold and the dusting of beard shadowing his chin. He was a handsome, complicated man but one she felt she could trust, one she could easily love. She thought of their nights together, sometimes tempestuously hot, other times incredibly tender. Biting on her lower lip, she told herself he wasn't the man for her. Theirs was destined to be one of those star-crossed affairs that could never develop into a lasting relationship.

She twisted the locket in her fingers as she watched Kurt climb into the truck. She tried not to notice the way his jeans fit tight around his long, muscular legs, or the angle of his jaw — rock hard and incredibly masculine. She refused to dwell on the fact that his jacket stretched over the shoulders she'd traced with her fingers as she'd made love to him. Oh, Lord, what was she doing?

It didn't feel right.

Something about the way the case was coming down felt disjointed, out of sync.

Two days had passed since Eric Brown had called and the police had taken Donahue into custody, and yet Striker had the niggling sensation that wouldn't let go of him that something was off. That he was missing something vital.

He stood on the porch of the cabin and stared into old-growth timber that reached to the sky. The air was fresh from a shower earlier. Residual raindrops slid earthward from the fronds of thick ferns and long needles. Earlier, as he'd sat in the broken-down porch swing, he'd spotted a doe and her fawns, two jackrabbits and a raccoon scuttling into the thickets of fir and spruce. The sun had been out earlier, but now was sinking fast and the gloom of night was closing in. Striker was restless, felt that same itch that warned him trouble was brewing. Big trouble.

He hankered for a cigarette though he'd given up the habit ten years earlier. Only in times of stress or after two beers did he ever experience the yen for a swift hit of nicotine. Since he hadn't had a drop of liquor in days, it had to be the stress of the situation. Maybe it was because both he and Randi were experiencing a bad case of cabin fever.

Even the baby was cranky. No doubt the little guy had picked up on the vibes within the cabin. During the days the tension between him and Randi had been so thick a machete would have had trouble hacking through it. And the nights had been worse. Excruciating. Sheer damn torture as he'd tried, and failed, to keep his hands off her. Though neither one of them admitted the wanting, it was there, between them, enticing and erotic, and each night they'd given in to the temptation, making love as intensely as if they both thought it would be the last time.

Which it should be, all things considered.

But the fire he felt for her, the blinding, searing passion, wasn't an emotion easily dismissed; especially not in the cold mountain nights when she was so close to him, as willing, as eager as he to touch and reconnect.

Just thinking of the passion between them caused a stiffening between his legs, a swelling that was so uncomfortable, he had to adjust himself.

Hell.

Just like a horny teenager.

He ran frustrated fingers through his hair.

Soon this would be over.

Yeah, and then what?

Are you just going to walk away?

He clenched his jaw so hard it ached, and

kicked a fir cone with enough force to send it shooting deep into the woods. Not that anything was going to end soon. Unbelievable as it might seem, it looked as if Randi might be right about her ex-lover. Donahue's alibi for the day she'd been run off the road was airtight. Unbreakable. Donahue's two best friends swore that all three of them had been together in a Spokane tavern at the time. Though the border town was close enough to the Idaho panhandle and not that far from Montana, the time it would have taken Donahue to make the round-trip made it near-impossible for the cowboy or either of his cohorts to have actually done the deed.

Coupled with his friends' dubious testimony, a bartender at the tavern remembered the nefarious trio. Two other guys playing pool that day also acknowledged that the boisterous bunch had been downing beers like water that afternoon and into the evening.

Striker leaned against the weathered porch railing. There wasn't much chance that Sam Donahue had forced Randi off the road that day.

Unless he'd paid someone to try to kill her.

Kurt couldn't let it go.

Because you want it to be Donahue. Admit it. The fact that he's a mean son of a bitch and the father of Randi's baby bugs the hell out of you. You don't like to think of Randi making love to Donahue or anyone else for that matter. Just the thought of it makes you want to punch Donahue's lights out. Geez, Striker, you'd better get out now. While you still can. The longer you're around her, the harder it's going to be to give her up.

Angry at the turn of his thoughts, he spat into the forest and rammed his hands deep into the back pockets of his jeans.

You have no right getting involved with her. She's your client and you don't want a woman fouling up your life. Especially not a woman with a kid. He thought of his own daughter and realized the pain he usually felt when he remembered her was fading. Oh, there were still plenty of memories, but they were no longer clouded in guilt. That seemed wrong. He could never forget the guilt he carried. And it stung like the bite of a whip when he realized that some of his pain had been eased by being near Randi's child. As if letting little Joshua into his heart allowed him to release the pain over Heather's loss.

"Kurt?"

The door creaked open and Randi appeared. Stupidly, his heart leaped at the sight of her.

Tousled red-brown locks, big eyes and a dusting of freckles assaulted him and he felt his gut tighten. She'd spent the morning on his computer working on a couple of new columns that she planned to e-mail when they reached a cybercafé, and now, smiling enough to show off impossibly white teeth, she looked incredible. As sexy and earthy as the surrounding forest.

"How's the baby?" he asked, his voice a tad hoarser than usual.

"Sleeping. Finally." Arms huddled around her as if to ward off the cold, she walked outside and he noticed how her jeans fit so snugly over her rounded hips. The weight she'd gained while pregnant had disappeared quickly because she'd been in the hospital, on IVs while in a coma; hence her inability to breast-feed, though she'd tried diligently once she'd awoken. So now she was slim and, if the little lines puckering her eyebrows could be believed, worried.

He felt the urge to wrap an arm over her shoulders, but didn't give in to the intimacy.

"Can we get out of here?" she asked.

"What? And leave all this luxury?" He forced a smile he didn't feel and noticed that her lips twitched despite the creases in her forehead.

"It'll be hard, I know. A sacrifice. But I think it's time."

"And go where?"

"Home."

"I'm not sure your condo is safe."

"I'm not talking about Seattle," she admitted, her brown eyes dark with thought. "I think I need to go home. Back to Montana. Until this is all sorted out. I'll call my editor and explain what's going on. He'll have to let me work from the ranch. Well, he won't have to, but I think he will."

"Wait a minute. I thought you were hellbent to start over. To prove yourself. Take command of your life again."

"Oh, I am. Believe me." She nodded as if to convince herself. "But I'm going to do it closer to my family." Staring at him, she inched her chin up in a gesture he'd come to recognize as pure unabashed McCafferty, a simple display of unbridled spirit, the kind of fortitude that made it impossible for her to walk away from a challenge. "Come on, Striker, let's get a move on."

He glanced around the cabin and decided she was right. It was time to return to Montana. This case had started there . . . and now it was time to end it. Whoever had first attacked Randi had done it when she'd attempted to go back to her roots at the Flying M. Somehow that had to be the key. Someone had felt threatened that she was returning. Someone didn't want her back at the ranch . . . Someone hated her enough to try to kill her and her unborn child. . . .

His mind clicked.

New images appeared.

The baby. Once again, Striker thought Joshua was the center of this maelstrom. Didn't children bring out the deepest of emotions? Hadn't he felt them himself?

It was possible that whoever had started the attacks on Randi had done so with a single, deadly purpose in mind that Kurt hadn't quite understood. Perhaps Striker, Randi, the McCaffertys and even Sam Donahue had been manipulated. If so . . . there was only one person who would take Randi's fame and pregnancy as a personal slap in the face. And Kurt felt certain he knew who the culprit was.

"What do you know about Patsy Donahue?" he asked suddenly.

Randi started. "Sam's wife, or ex-wife, or whatever she is?"

"Yeah."

"Not a lot." Lifting a shoulder, Randi said, "Patsy was a year ahead of me in high school, the family didn't have much money and she got married right after she graduated, to her first boyfriend, Ned Lefever."

"You weren't friends with Patsy?"

"Hardly." Randi shook her head. "She never liked me much. Her dad had worked for mine, then her folks split up and I think she even had a crush on Slade, before Ned . . . well, it's complicated."

"Explain. We've got time."

"I won some riding competition once and edged her out and . . . oh, this is really so high school, but Ned asked me to the prom. He and Patsy were broken up at the time."

"Did you go?"

"To the prom, yes. But not with Ned. I already had a date. And I wasn't interested in Ned Lefever. I thought he was a blowhard and a braggart." Randi rested a hand against the battle-scarred railing as she rolled back the years. "It was weird, though. All night long, during the dance, I was on the receiving end of looks that could kill. From Patsy. As if I was to blame for Ned's —" She froze. "Oh, God, you think Patsy's behind the attacks, don't you?"

Kurt's eyes held hers. "I'd bet my life on it."

CHAPTER TWELVE

"How could she let herself get tangled up with the likes of Donahue?" Matt grumbled to his brother as he uncinched Diablo Rojo's saddle. For his efforts, the Appaloosa swung his head around in hopes of taking a nip out of Matt's leg. Deftly Matt sidestepped the nip. "You never learn, do you?" he muttered to the fiery colt.

Rojo snorted, stamping a foot in the barn and tossing his devilish head. Matt, Slade and Larry Todd, the recently rehired foreman, had been riding nearly all day, searching for strays, calves who might have been separated from the herd in the cold Montana winter. Spring was still a few months off and the weather had been fierce since Christmas, snow drifting to the eaves of some of the outbuildings.

Larry had already taken off, but Slade and Matt were cooling down their horses now that three bawling, near-frozen calves had been reunited with their mothers. The barn was warm and smelled of dust, dry straw and horseflesh. The same smells Matt had grown up with. Harold, their father's crippled old spaniel, was lying near the tack-room door, his tail thumping whenever Matt glanced in his direction.

Slade unhooked The General's bridle and the big gelding pushed against Slade's chest with his great head. He rubbed the horse's crooked white blaze and said, "I don't think Randi planned on getting involved with Donahue." The brothers had been discussing their sister's situation most of the day, hoping to find some answers to all of their questions.

"Hell, the man was married. I bet Patsy put up one helluva ruckus when she found out."

Slade nodded.

"She always was a hothead. She never liked Randi, either, not since Randi beat her out of some competition when they were in high school."

"What competition?" Slade scooped oats from a barrel with an old coffee can. The General, always eager for food, nickered softly. As Slade poured the grain into the manger, the old chestnut was already chomping.

"I can't remember. I wasn't around, but Dad mentioned it once. Something about horse racing, yeah, barrel racing, when they were kids. Randi beat Patsy, and Patsy did something to her at school the next week."

Slade began rubbing The General down. "Wasn't that Patsy Ellis? Jesus, I think she had a thing for me once."

"You always think women are interested in you."

"Don't tell Jamie."

"Right." Matt was feeding Rojo. Thankfully the colt was finally more interested in food than in taking a nip out of Matt's hide. "That was her maiden name. Right after high school she married Ned Lefever. A few years later they were divorced and a while after that she took up with Donahue, married him. It must really have teed her off that he ended up cheating on her with an old rival."

"A woman scorned," Slade muttered as the barn door opened and Kelly, her eyes bright, her cheeks nearly as red as the strands of hair escaping from her stocking cap, burst inside. Harold gave off a gruff bark.

"Shh," Kelly reprimanded, though she bent over to pat the old dog's head. Snow had collected on her eyelashes and was melting on her skin. To Matt, as always, she looked sweet and sexy and was the most incredible woman to walk this earth. "I just got a call from Striker," she announced breathlessly as she straightened. "He and Randi are on their way back here, and guess what? They think Patsy Donahue is behind all this."

Matt and Slade exchanged glances.

"I've already checked with Espinoza, and the police are looking for her, just to ask her some questions. I put a call in to Charlie Caldwell's ex-girlfriend and guess who handed her over the keys to the maroon Ford van that edged Randi's Jeep off the road? Good old Patsy."

Slade's grin moved from one side of his face to the other. "Your husband and I had just come up with the same idea," he said.

"No way."

"Honest to God." Matt held up a gloved hand as if he was being sworn in at a trial.

"Great. Now you can both be honorary detectives and form your own posse or something."

Matt tossed aside the brush and walked out of Diablo Rojo's stall. "Don't I at least get a kiss for being so smart?" he teased.

"If you were so smart why didn't you come up with this idea months ago and save us all a lot of grief. Forget the kiss, Mc-Cafferty." She winked at him and his heart galumphed. He'd never figured out why she got to him so, how when she walked into the room, everything else melted into the background. "Besides," she said coyly, "I expected smart when I married you."

"And good-looking and sexy?" he asked, and heard his brother guffaw from The General's stall.

"Minimum requirements," she teased. Matt dropped a kiss on her forehead and molded his glove over the slight curvature of her belly where his unborn child was growing. "Come on, you good-looking, sexy son of a gun," she began, pulling on the tabs of his jeans.

"On my way," Slade intercepted.

"I think she was talking to me." Matt shot his brother a look that could cut through steel.

"Both of you!" Kelly insisted, backing toward the door. "Let's go have a little heart-to-heart with Patsy Donahue."

"I think you'd better leave that to the police," Matt said.

"I was the police, remember?"

"Yeah, but now you're my wife, the mother of my not-yet-born child and Patsy could be dangerous."

"I'm not afraid."

"Spoken like a true McCafferty," Slade said as he slipped from The General's stall and tested the latch to make certain it was secure. "But maybe you should leave this to the Brothers McCafferty."

"We're like the Three Musketeers," Matt said.

"I won't say the obvious about a certain trio of stooges," she baited, and for her insolence, Matt whipped her off her feet and hugged her.

"Sometimes, woman, you try my patience."

She laughed and winked up at him with sassy insolence as he set her on her feet.

"Leave this to the men," Matt insisted as he held the barn door open and a blast of icy Montana wind swept inside.

"In your dreams, boys." Kelly adjusted the scarf around her neck as she trudged through the snow toward the ranch house. Not far from the barn stood the remains of the stables, blackened and charred, in stark contrast to the pristine mantle of white and a glaring reminder of the trouble that had beset the family ever since Randi's fateful drive east. "Look," Kelly said, sending her husband a determined glare. "I've been involved with this case since the beginning.

Patsy Donahue is mine."

"Guess what?" Kurt asked as he clicked off the cell phone. They were driving east through Idaho, closing in on the western Montana border. Night was coming and fast, no moon or stars visible through the thick clouds blanketing the mountains. "That was Kelly. She and Espinoza and your brothers went over to Patsy Donahue's place."

"Let me guess." Randi adjusted the zipper of her jacket. "Patsy is missing."

"Hasn't been at her house for days, if the stacked-up mail is to be believed."

"Great." Randi was disheartened. Would this nightmare never end? It was unbelievable to think that one woman could wreak such havoc, be so dangerous or so desperate. Could Patsy hate her that much as to try to kill her? Kill her baby? Harm her brothers?

"I just don't get it," Randi said as she turned toward the back seat to check on Joshua. The baby, lulled by the hum of the truck's engine and the gentle motion of the spinning wheels, was sleeping soundly, nestled in his car seat. "Why take it out on the ranch . . . I mean, if she had a thing against me, why harm my brothers?"

"The way I figure it, Thorne's plane crash was an accident. Patsy wasn't involved in that. But the attacks on you were personal and the fire in the stable was to keep you frightened, maintain a level of terror."

"Well, it worked. Slade nearly lost his life and the livestock . . . Dear God, why put the animals in jeopardy?" She bit her lip and stared at the few flakes of snow slowly falling from a darkening sky. Sagebrush and scrub pine poked through the white, snow-covered landscape, but the road was clear, the headlights of Striker's truck illuminating the ribbon of frigid pavement stretching before them.

"She's angry. Not just at you but at your family. Probably because she doesn't have much of one. Besides, you own the lion's share of the ranch. She must've figured that hurting the ranch and hurting your brothers was hurting you." He flicked a look through the rearview mirror. "I just feel like a fool for not seeing it sooner."

"No one did," she admitted, though that thought was dismal. Maybe when they arrived at the ranch, Patsy would be in custody. Silently Randi crossed her fingers. "So what's going to happen to Sam?"

"He's being questioned. Just because he wasn't responsible for harming you doesn't

217

mean he's not a criminal. If you testify about his animal abuse, illegal betting and his throwing of the rodeo competitions, we'll have a good start in bringing him to justice. There's no telling what the authorities will dig up now that they've been pointed in the right direction."

"Of course I'll testify."

"It won't be easy. He'll be sitting at the defense table, staring at you, hearing every word."

"I know how it works," she retorted, then softened her tone as they passed through a small timber town where only a few lights were winking from the houses scattered near the road and a sawmill stood idle, elevators and sheds ghostlike and hulking around a gravel parking lot and a pile of sawdust several stories high. "But the truth is the truth," Randi continued, "no matter who's listening. Believe me, I'm over Sam Donahue. I would have taken all of the evidence I'd gathered against him to the rodeo commission and the authorities if I hadn't been sidetracked and sent to the hospital." She leaned back against the seat as the miles sped beneath the truck's tires. "I had worried about it. Wondered how I would face Joshua's father. But that's over. Now I'm sure I can face him. The way I look at it, Sam Donahue was the sperm donor that created my son. It takes a lot more to be a real father."

The baby started coughing and Randi turned to him. Kurt glanced back as well. Joshua's little face was bright red, his eyes glassy. "How much longer until we get to Grand Hope?"

"Probably eight or nine hours."

"I'm worried about the baby."

"I am, too," Kurt admitted as he glared at the road ahead.

Joshua, as if he knew they were talking about him, gave off a soft little whimper.

"Give me the cell phone," Randi said. She couldn't stand it another minute. Joshua wasn't getting any better; in fact, he was worsening, and her worries were going into overdrive. Kurt handed her the phone, and she, trying to calm her case of nerves, dialed the ranch house as she plugged in the adapter to the cigarette lighter.

"Hello. Flying M Ranch," Juanita said, her accent barely detectible.

Randi nearly melted with relief at the sound of the housekeeper's voice. "Juanita, this is Randi."

"Oh, Miss Randi! *¡Dios!,* where are you? And the *niño.* How is he?"

"That's why I'm calling. We're on our way

back to the ranch, but Joshua's feverish and I'm worried. Is Nicole there?"

"Oh, no. She is with your brother and they are at their new house, talking with the builder."

"Do you have her pager number?"

"*¡Sí!*" Quickly, Juanita rattled off not only the telephone number for Nicole's pager, but Thorne's cell phone as well. "Call them now, and you keep that baby warm." Juanita muttered something in Spanish that Randi interpreted as a prayer before hanging up. Immediately Randi dialed Thorne's cell and once he answered, she insisted on talking to his wife. Nicole had admitted Randi into the hospital after the accident, and with the aid of Dr. Arnold, a pediatrician on the staff of St. James, had taken care of Joshua during the first tenuous hours of his young life.

Now, she said, "Keep fluids in him, watch his temperature, keep him warm, and I'll put a call into Gus Arnold. He's still your pediatrician, right?"

"Yes."

"Then you're in good hands. Gus is the best. I'll make sure that either he or one of his partners meets us at the hospital. When do you think you'll get here?"

"Kurt's saying about eight or nine hours.

I'll call when we're closer."

"I'll be there," Nicole assured her, and Randi was thankful for her sister-in-law's reassurances. "Now, how are you doing?"

"Fine," Randi said, though that was a bit of a stretch. "Eager to get home, though."

"I'll bet — oh! What . . . ?" Her voice faded a bit as if she'd turned her head, and Randi heard only part of a conversation before Nicole said, "Look, your brother is dying to talk to you. Humor him, would you?"

"Sure."

"Randi?" Thorne's voice boomed over the phone and Randi felt the unlikely urge to break down and cry. "What the hell's going on?" Thorne demanded. "Kelly seems to think that Patsy Donahue is the one behind all this trouble."

"It looks that way."

"And now Patsy's gone missing? Why the hell hasn't Striker found her?"

"Because he's been babysitting me," Randi said, suddenly defensive. No one could fault Kurt; not even her brothers. From the corner of her eye Randi noticed Kurt wince, his hands gripping the steering wheel even harder. "He's got someone on it."

"Hell's bells, so does Bob Espinoza, but

no one seems to be able to find her. It's time to call in the FBI and the CIA and the state police and the damn federal marshals!"

"She'll be found," Randi assured him, though she, herself, doubted her words. "It's just a matter of time."

"It can't happen soon enough to suit me." He paused, then, "Tell me about J.R. How is he?"

"*Joshua's* running a temperature and has a cold. I'm meeting Nicole at St. James Hospital."

"I'll be there, too."

"You? A big corporate executive? Don't you have better things to do?" she teased, and he laughed.

"Yeah, right now I'm discussing the kind of toilet to go into the new house. Believe me, it's a major decision. Nicole's leaning toward the low-flow, water-conservation model, but I think we should go standard."

"I think I've heard enough," Randi said, giggling. Some of her tension ebbed a bit.

"You and me both. We haven't even started with colors yet. I'm leaning toward white."

"Big surprise, oh conservative one."

He chuckled. "Well, it's too damn dark and cold to make many more decisions tonight. That's what happens when you're married to a doctor who works sixty or seventy hours a week and then gets detained at the hospital."

"Poor baby," Randi mocked.

"Uh-oh, they need me," he said, but his voice was fading, the connection breaking up. "I think . . . going to check into . . . sinks and . . . see you in a few hours . . ."

"Thorne? Are you there?"

Only crackle.

"I'm losing you!"

"Randi?" Thorne's voice was suddenly strong.

"Yeah?"

"I'm glad you're coming home."

"Me, too," she said, and her throat caught as she envisioned her oldest half brother with his black hair and intense gray eyes. She imagined the concern etched on his strong features. "Give my love to . . ." but the connection was lost, as they were deep in the mountains. Reluctantly, she clicked the cell phone off.

"He wants to know why I haven't tracked Patsy down yet," Striker surmised, his lips blade thin.

"He wants to know why *no one's* tracked Patsy down. Your name came up, yes, but so did Detective Espinoza's, along with every government agency known to man. You have to understand one thing about Thorne. He gives an order and he expects immediate, and I mean im-me-di-ate, results. Which, of course, is impossible."

"I'm with him, though," Kurt said. "The sooner we nail Patsy Donahue, the better."

Randi wanted to agree with him, but there was a part of her that balked, for she knew that the minute Patsy was located and locked away, Kurt would be gone. Out of her life forever. Her heart twisted and she wondered how she'd ever let him go. It was silly really. She'd only known him for a month or so and only intensely for a week.

And yet she would miss him.

More than she'd ever thought possible.

This entire midnight run to Montana seemed doomed. Joshua's fever was worsening, there was talk of a blizzard ahead, and somewhere in the night, Patsy Donahue was planning another attack. Randi could feel it in her bones. She shivered.

"Cold?" Kurt adjusted the heater.

"I'm fine." But it was a lie. They both knew it. Every time a vehicle approached, Randi tensed, half expecting the driver to crank on the wheel and sideswipe Striker's truck. Silently she prayed that they'd reach Grand Hope without any incident, that her baby would recover quickly and that Kurt

Striker would be a part of her life forever. It was a hard fact to face, one she'd denied for a long time, but no protests to herself or anyone else could overcome the God's honest truth: Randi McCafferty had fallen in love with Kurt Striker.

Patsy drummed gloved fingers on the wheel of her stolen rig, an older-model SUV that had been parked for hours at a bar on the interstate in Idaho. No one would be able to connect her to the theft. She'd ditched her van on an abandoned road near Dalles, Oregon, gotten on a bus and traveled east until the truck stop, where she'd located the rig and switched license plates with some she'd lifted while in Seattle. By the time anyone pieced together what she'd done, it would be too late. She was behind Striker's pickup, probably by an hour or so, but she figured she could make up the distance. It would take time, but eventually she'd be able to catch the bitch.

And then there would be hell to pay.

Her speedometer hovered near seventy, but she pushed on the accelerator and pumped up the volume on the radio. An old Rolling Stones tune reverberated through the speakers. Mick Jagger was screaming about getting no satisfaction. Usually Patsy identified with the song. But not tonight. Tonight she intended to get all the satisfaction she'd been lacking in recent years.

The SUV flew down the freeway. Patsy didn't let up for a second. She'd driven in dry snow all her life and felt no fear.

By daybreak her mission would be accomplished.

Randi McCafferty and anyone stupid enough to be with the bitch would be dead.

CHAPTER THIRTEEN

The baby wouldn't stop crying.

Nothing Randi did stopped the wails coming from the back seat and Striker felt helpless. He drove as fast as he dared while Randi twisted in her seat, trying to feed Joshua or comfort him, but the baby was having none of it.

Striker gritted his teeth and hoped that the baby's fever hadn't climbed higher. He thought of the pain of losing a child and knew he had to do something, *anything* to prevent the little guy's life from slipping away.

He gunned the pickup ever faster, but the terrain had become rough, with sharp turns and steep grades as they drove deep into the foothills of the Montana mountains.

"He's still very warm," Randi said, touching her son's cheek.

"We'll be there in less than an hour," Striker assured her. "Hang in there."

"If he will," Randi whispered hoarsely, and it tore his heart to hear her desperation.

"I think it's better that he's crying rather than listless," Striker offered, knowing it was little consolation.

"I guess. Maybe we should get off and try to find a clinic."

"In the rinky-dink towns around here? At three in the morning? St. James is the nearest hospital. Just call Nicole and tell her we'll be there in forty-five minutes."

"All right." She reached for the phone just as Striker glanced in the rearview mirror. Headlights were bearing down on them and fast, even though he was doing near sixty on the straight parts of this curving, treacherous section of interstate. At the corners he'd had to slow to near thirty and he'd spotted the vehicle behind him gaining, taking the corners wide. "Hang on," he said.

"What?"

"I've got someone on my tail and closing fast. It would be best if I let them go around me." He saw a wide spot in the road, slowed down, and the other vehicle shot past, a blur of dark paint and shiny wheels.

"We'll probably catch up to him rolled over in the ditch ahead."

"Great," she whispered.

He took a turn a little fast and the wheels

slid, so he slowed a bit. As he passed by an old logging road, he thought he saw a dark vehicle. Idling. No headlights or taillights visible, but exhaust fogging the cold night air. The same fool who'd passed them? The hairs on the back of his neck lifted.

It was too dark to be certain and he told himself that he was just being paranoid. No one in his right mind would be sitting in their rig in the dark. His gut clenched. Of course no one in his *right mind* would be there. But what about a woman no longer in control of her faculties, a woman hellbent for revenge, a woman like Patsy Donahue?

No way, Striker. You're tired and jumping at shadows. That's all.

Pull yourself together.

He peered into the rearview mirror and saw nothing in the darkness. No headlights beyond the snow flurries . . . or did he? Was there a vehicle barreling after him, one with no headlights, one using his taillights to guide it? His mouth was suddenly desert dry. The image took shape then faded. His mind playing tricks on him. Nothing more. God, he hoped so.

"What?" Randi asked, sensing his apprehension. The baby was still crying, but more softly now. The road was steep and winding and he cut his speed in order to keep the truck on the asphalt.

"Look behind us. See anything?"

Again Randi twisted in her seat and peered through the window over the back of the king cab. She squinted hard. "No. Why?"

He scowled, saw his own reflection in the mirror. "I thought I saw something. A shadow."

"A shadow?"

"Of a car. I though someone might be following us with his lights out."

"In this terrain? In the dark?" she asked, and then sucked in her breath and stared hard through the window. "I don't see anything."

"Good." He felt a second's relief. This would be the worst place to encounter danger. The road was barely two lanes with steep mountains on one side and a slim guardrail on the other. Beyond the barrier was a sheer cliff where only the tops of trees were visible in the glare of his headlights as he swept around the corners.

Randi didn't stop looking through the window, searching the darkness, and he could tell by the way she held on to the back of the seat, her white-knuckled grasp a death grip, that, she, too, was concerned.

His hands began to sweat on the wheel, but he told himself they were all right, they would make it, they only had a few more miles. He thought of how, in the past few weeks, he'd fallen for Randi McCafferty hook, line and proverbial sinker. With a glance in her direction, his heart filled. He couldn't imagine life without her or without little Joshua. As much as he'd sworn after Heather's death never to get close to a woman or a child again, he'd broken his own pact with himself. And it was too late to change his mind. His stubborn heart just wouldn't let him. Maybe it was time to tell her. To be honest. Let her know how he felt.

Why?

Come on, Striker, are you so full of yourself to imagine she loves you? And what about the kid? Didn't you swear off fatherhood for good? What are you doing considering becoming a father again? Why would you set yourself up for that kind of heartache all over again? Remember Heather? Do you really think you have it in you to be a parent?

The arguments tore through his mind. Nonetheless, he had to tell her. "Randi?"

"What?" She was still staring out the back window.

"About the last few nights —"

"Please," she said, refusing to look his way.

"You don't have to explain. Neither of us planned what happened."

"But you should know how I feel."

He noticed her tense. She swallowed hard. "Maybe I don't want to," she whispered before she gasped. "Oh, God, no!"

"What?"

"I think . . . I think there *is* someone back there. Every once in a while I see an image and then it fades into the background. You don't think . . ."

Kurt stared into the rearview mirror. "Hell." He saw it too. The outline of a dark vehicle without its lights on, driving blind, bearing down, swerving carelessly from one side of the road to the other and then melding with the night. He pressed hard on the accelerator. "Keep your eye on it and call the police."

She reached for the phone. Dialed 911.

Nothing.

"Damn."

She tried again and was rewarded by a beeping of the cell. "No signal," she said, staring through the window as the baby cried.

"Keep trying." Kurt took a corner too fast, the wheels spun and they swung wide, into the oncoming lane. "Damn it."

"It's getting closer!"

Kurt saw the vehicle now, looming behind them, dangerously close as they screeched around corners. "Hell."

"Do you think it's Patsy?"

"Unless there's some other nutcase running loose."

"Oh, God . . ." Randi sounded frantic. "What's she going to do?"

"I don't know." But he had only to think of the accident where Randi was forced off the road to come up with a horrific scenario.

Randi punched out the number of the police again. "The call's going through! Where are we? I'll have to give our location . . . oh, no . . . lost the signal again."

"Hit redial!" Kurt ordered. A sign at the edge of the road warned of a steep downgrade.

"Maybe you should just slow down," Randi said. "Force her to slow."

"What if she's got a gun. A rifle?"

"A gun?"

The vehicle switched on its lights suddenly and seemed to leap forward.

Kurt swung to the inside, toward the mountain.

The SUV bore down on them.

A sharp corner loomed. A sign said that maximum speed for the corner was thirty-five. The needle of his speedometer was pushing sixty. He shifted down. Pumped the brakes. Squealed around the corner, fishtailing.

The SUV didn't give up. "She's getting closer," Randi cried as she kept redialing. "Oh, God!"

Bam!

The nose of the trailing vehicle struck hard as Kurt hit a pothole. The truck shuddered, snaking to the guardrail, wheels bouncing over a washboard of asphalt and gravel. Kurt rode out the slide, easing into it, only changing direction at the last minute. His heart was pounding, his body sweating. He couldn't lose Randi and the baby!

"Hello! Hello! This is an emergency!" Randi cried, as if she'd gotten through to police dispatch. "Someone's trying to kill us. We're on the interstate in northern Montana." She yelled their approximate location and the highway number, then swore as the connection failed.

Thud!

Again they were battered from behind.

The front wheel hit a patch of ice and the truck began to spin, circling in what seemed like slow motion. Kurt struggled with the steering wheel, saw the guardrail and the black void beyond. Gritting his teeth, trying to keep the truck on the road, he felt the fender slam into the railing and heard the horrid groan of metal ripping. Over it all the baby cried and Randi screamed. "Come on, come on," Kurt said between clenched teeth, willing the pickup to stay on the road, his shoulders aching. He couldn't lose the woman he loved, nor her child. Not now. Not this way. Not again.

"Oh my God, look out!" Randi cried, but it was too late.

The SUV hit the truck midspin, plowing into the passenger side with a sickening crash and the rending of steel. Kurt's fingers clenched over the wheel, but the truck didn't respond. The SUV's bumper locked to the truck and together the two vehicles spun down the road, faster and faster. Trees and darkness flashed by in a blur.

Randi screamed.

The baby wailed.

Kurt swore. "Hold on!" The two melded vehicles slammed into the side of the mountain and ricocheted across the road with enough force to send the entangled trucks through the guardrail and into the black void beyond.

Somewhere there was a bell ringing . . . steady . . . never getting any louder . . . just a simple bleating. It was so irritating. *Answer the phone, for God's sake . . . answer it!* Randi's head ached, her body felt as if she'd been beaten from head to toe, there was an awful taste in her mouth and . . . She opened an eye and blinked. Everything was so white and blinding.

"Can you hear me? Randi?" Someone shined a light into her eyes and she recoiled. The voice was a woman's. A voice she should recognize. Randi closed her eyes. Wanted to sleep again. She was in a bed with rails . . . a hospital bed . . . how did she get here? Vaguely she remembered the smell of burning rubber and fresh pine . . . there had been red and blue lights and her family . . . all standing around . . . and Kurt leaning over her, whispering he loved her, his face battered and bruised and bleeding . . . Or had it been a dream? Kurt . . . where the hell was Kurt? And the baby? Joshua. Oh God! Her eyes flew open and she tried to speak.

"Jo . . . Joshua?"

"The baby's okay."

Everything was blurry for a minute before she focused and saw Nicole standing in the room. Another doctor was examining her, but her eyes locked with those of her sister-in-law. Memories of the horrible night and the car wreck assailed her.

"Joshua is at home. With Juanita. As soon as you're released you can be with him."

She let out her breath, relieved that her child had survived.

"You're lucky," the doctor said, and Nicole was nodding behind him. *Lucky? Lucky?* There didn't seem anything the least bit lucky about what happened.

"Kurt?" she managed to get out though her throat was raw, her words only a whisper.

"He's all right."

Thank God. Slowly turning her head, Randi looked around. The hospital room was stark. An IV dripped fluid into her wrist, a monitor showed her heartbeat and kept up the beeping she'd heard as she'd awoken. Flowers stood in vases on a windowsill.

"I . . . I want to see . . . my baby . . . and . . . and Striker."

"You've been in the hospital two days, Randi," Nicole said. "With a concussion and a broken wrist. J.R., er, Joshua, had a bad cold but didn't suffer anything from the accident. Luckily there was an ambulance only fifteen minutes away from the site of the accident. Police dispatch had gotten your message, so they were able to get to you fairly quickly."

"Where's Kurt?"

Nicole cleared her throat. "Gone."

Randi's heart sank. He'd already left. The ache within her grew.

"He had some eye damage and a dislocated shoulder."

"And he just left."

Little lines gathered between Nicole's eyebrows. "Yes. I know that he went to Seattle to see a specialist. An optic neurologist."

Randi forced the words over her tongue. "How bad is his vision?"

"I don't know."

"Is he blind?"

"I really don't know, Randi."

She felt as if her sister-in-law was holding back. "Kurt's not coming back, is he?"

Nicole took her hand and twined strong fingers between Randi's. "I'm not certain, but since you're going to ask, if I were a betting woman, I'd have to say 'No, I don't think so.' He and Thorne had words. Now, please, take your doctor's advice and rest. You have a baby waiting for you at the Flying M and three half brothers who are anxious for you to come home." Nicole squeezed Randi's fingers and Randi closed her eyes. So they'd survived.

"What about Patsy?" she asked.

"In custody. As luck would have it, she got away unscathed."

The doctor attending her cleared his throat. "You really do need to rest," he said.

"Like hell." She scrabbled for the button to raise her head. "I want to get out of here and see my baby and —" Excruciating pain splintered through her brain. She sank back on her pillow. "Maybe you're right," she admitted. She had to get well. For Joshua.

And what about Kurt? Her heart ached at the thought that she might never see him again. Damn it, she couldn't just let him walk away.

Or could she?

Three days later she was released from the hospital and reunited with her family. Joshua was healthy again, and it felt good to hold him in her arms, to smell his baby-clean scent. Juanita was in her element, fussing and clucking over Randi and the baby, generally bossing her brothers around and running the house.

Larry Todd seemed to have forgiven Randi for letting him go, though he insisted on a signed contract for his work, and even Bill Withers, after hearing of the accident, had agreed to allow Randi to write her column from Montana. "Just don't let it get out," he said over the phone. "People around here might get the idea that I'm a softie."

"I wouldn't lose any sleep over it if I were you," Randi said before hanging up and deciding to tackle her oldest brother. She checked on the baby and found him sleeping in his crib, then, with her arm in a sling, made her way downstairs. The smells of chocolate and maple wafted from the kitchen where Juanita was baking.

Though Slade and Matt were nowhere to be found, she located Thorne at his desk in the den. He sat at his computer, a neglected cup of coffee at his side. No doubt he was working on some corporate buyout, a lawsuit, the ever-changing plans for his house, or concocting some new way to make his next million. Randi didn't care what he was doing. He could damn well be interrupted.

"I heard you gave Striker a bad time." She was on pain medication but was steady enough on her feet to loom above the desk in her bathrobe and slippers.

Thorne looked up at her and smiled. "You heard right."

"Blamed him for what happened to me and Joshua."

"I might have come down on him a little hard," her brother admitted with uncharacteristic equanimity.

"You had no right, you know. He did his best."

"And it wasn't good enough. You were nearly killed. So was Joshua."

"We survived. Because of Kurt."

A smile twitched at the corners of his mouth. "I figured that out."

"You did?"

"Yep." He reached into his drawer and held out two pieces of a torn check. "Striker wouldn't accept any payment. He felt bad about what happened."

"And you made it worse."

"Nah." He leaned back in the desk chair until it squeaked and tented his hands as he looked up at her. "Well, okay, I did, but I changed my mind."

"What good does that do?"

"A lot," he said.

She narrowed her eyes. "You're up to something."

"Making amends."

"That sounds ominous."

"I don't think so." He glanced to the window and Randi heard it then, the rumble of an engine. "Looks like our brothers are back."

"They've been away?"

"Mmm. Come on." He climbed out of his

desk chair and walked with her to the front door. She looked out the window and saw Matt and Slade climb out of a Jeep. But there was another man with them and in a pulse beat she recognized Kurt. Her heart nearly jumped from her chest and she threw open the door, nearly tripping on Harold as she raced across the porch.

"Wait!" Thorne cried, but she was already running along the path beaten in the snow, her slippers little protection, her robe billowing in the cold winter air.

"Kurt!" she yelled, and only then noticed the eye-patch. He turned and a smile split his square jaw. Without thinking, she flung herself into his arms. "God, I missed you," she whispered and felt tears stream from her eyes. His face was bruised, his good eye slightly swollen. "Why did you leave?"

"I thought it was best." His voice was husky. Raw. The arm around her strong and steady.

"Then you thought wrong." She kissed him hard and felt his mouth mold to hers, his body flex against her.

When he finally lifted his head, he was smiling. "That's what your brothers said." He glanced up at Thorne who had followed Randi outside. He stiffened slightly.

"I'm glad you're back," Thorne said. "I

made a mistake."

"What? You're actually apologizing?" Randi, still in Kurt's arms, looked over her shoulder. "This," she said to Kurt, "is a red-letter day. Thorne McCafferty never, and I mean, never, admits he's wrong."

"Amen," Matt said.

"Right on," Slade agreed.

Thorne's jaw clenched. "Will you stay?" he asked Striker.

"I'll see. Give me a second, will you." He looked at all the brothers, who suddenly found reasons to retreat to the house. "It's freezing out here and you're hurt . . ." He touched her wrist. "So I'll keep this simple. Randi McCafferty, will you marry me?"

"Wh-what?"

"I mean it. Ever since I met you . . . and that kid of yours, life hasn't been the same."

"I can't believe this," she said breathlessly.

"Do. Believe, Randi."

Her heart squeezed. Fresh tears streamed from her eyes.

"Marry me."

"Yes. Yes! Yes!" She threw her good arm around his neck and silently swore she'd never let go.

EPILOGUE

"I do," Randi said as she stood beneath an arbor of roses. Kurt was with her, the preacher was saying the final words and Kelly was holding Joshua as Randi's brothers stood next to Kurt and her sisters-in-law surrounded her. The backyard of the ranch was filled with guests and the summer sun cast golden rays across the acres of land.

It had been over a year since John Randall had passed on. The new stable was finished, if not painted, and Thorne and his family had moved into their house. Both Nicole and Kelly were nearly at term in their pregnancies.

"I give to you Mr. and Mrs. Kurt Striker . . ." The preacher's final words echoed across the acres and somewhere from Big Meadow a horse let out a loud nicker.

Randi gazed up at her bridegroom and her heart swelled. He had healed from the accident, only a small scar near one eye reminding her that his peripheral vision had been compromised.

Both Patsy and Sam Donahue had been tried and convicted and were serving time. Sam had agreed to give up all parental rights and Kurt was working with an attorney to legally adopt Joshua.

They lived here at the ranch house and Randi was able to keep working, though Kurt thought she should give up her column entitled "Solo" and start writing for young marrieds.

"Toast!" Matt cried as she and Kurt walked toward the table where a sweating ice sculpture of two running horses was melting and pink champagne bubbled from a fountain.

"To the newlyweds," Thorne said.

Randi smiled and fingered the locket at her throat. Once it had held a picture of her father and son. Now John Randall had been replaced by a small snapshot of her husband.

"To my wife," Kurt said, and touched the rim of his glass to hers.

"And my husband."

She swallowed a glass of champagne and greeted their guests. Never had she felt such joy. Never had she felt so complete. She held her son and danced on a makeshift floor as the band began to play and shadows began to crawl across the vast acres of the Flying M.

"I love you," Kurt whispered to her and she laughed.

"You'd better! Forever!"

"That's an awful long time."

"I know. Isn't it wonderful?" she teased.

"The best." He kissed her and held her for a long minute, then they walked through the guests and she saw her brothers with their wives . . . Finally all of the McCafferty children were married. As John Randall McCafferty had wanted. More grandchildren were on the way.

She could almost hear her father saying to her, "Good goin', Randi girl. About time you tied the knot."

As she danced with her new husband, she could feel her father's presence and she didn't doubt for a second that had he been here, the old man would've been proud.

Another generation of McCaffertys was on its way.

ABOUT THE AUTHOR

Lisa Jackson is the bestselling author of over sixty books, ranging from historical romances to romantic suspense to thrillers. Her work has appeared on the *New York Times, USA TODAY* and *Publishers Weekly* bestseller lists. Look for more classic Lisa Jackson stories coming soon from HQN.

The employees of Thorndike Press hope you have enjoyed this Large Print book. All our Thorndike and Wheeler Large Print titles are designed for easy reading, and all our books are made to last. Other Thorndike Press Large Print books are available at your library, through selected bookstores, or directly from us.

For information about titles, please call:
(800) 223-1244

or visit our Web site at:
www.gale.com/thorndike
www.gale.com/wheeler

To share your comments, please write:
Publisher
Thorndike Press
295 Kennedy Memorial Drive
Waterville, ME 04901